I0691043

The Interpretation of Cakes

The Interpretation of Cakes

Allan Tegg

PUNCHER & WATTMANN

© Allan Tegg 2023

This book is copyright. Apart from any fair dealing for the purposes of study and research, criticism, review or as otherwise permitted under the Copyright Act, no part may be reproduced by any process without written permission. Inquiries should be made to the publisher.

First published in 2023
Published by Puncher & Wattmann
PO Box 279
Waratah NSW 2298

info@puncherandwattmann.com

NATIONAL
LIBRARY
OF AUSTRALIA

A catologue record for this book is available from The National Library of Australia.

ISBN   9781922571953

Cover design by Miranda Douglas
Printed by Lightning Source International

For Risé

Contents

♛ Prologue

There is a point, three kilometres west of the city, where Sydney Harbour transforms into the Parramatta River. It's the spot where the container ships and cruise liners give way to the small craft the locals use for a day's outing. I was drawn to that place when I was making my own transition—from psychotherapist to retiree. I planned to sit in the foreshore park and catch up with the novels I'd not had time to read. My unconscious quickly told me it had other ideas. I would not be settling into my final years.

I had spent my working life witnessing the brute strength of a psyche demanding to be heard. It forces people into deep depressions. It turns lives upside down, frustrating every attempt to put things back together. There is no escape. In the end, you will listen, or live in constant emotional pain.

I was one of the lucky ones. All I needed was a gentle distraction. Each day, I looked over the bay and was mesmerised by the scene. My psyche would then get to work. I meandered through my childhood, and revisited foreign cities. There were moments of crippling illness, and successes on the sporting field. I was allowed to watch these reminiscences with pleasant detachment. There were no tears, or powerful feelings of joy. I did not even feel shame at the silly things I had done. After spending a few hours with these recollections, I would wander back home. I felt deeply satisfied, as if I had done a good morning's work. I had no idea my unconscious had a strategy. It was keeping me in a reflective state of mind, preparing me to hear what it wanted to tell me.

One day, a mullet jumped out of the water, breaking my stream of consciousness. Just as the fish splashed back into the bay, a thought rose to the centre of my brain. "If you really want to retire, you have to stop thinking like a psychotherapist. Stop ruminating on who you are and why you do the things you do. Start taking the world at face value. That's when you've genuinely downed tools. Then you can get on with your reading, if that's what you still want to do." I stopped gazing at the water and looked down at my hands. They were clasped tightly in front of my chest. "That's the maddest idea ever," I thought.

Over forty years, I had trained myself to seek out the deeper meanings that were cheekily hidden in my patients' words. I had taught my intuition to sniff out the clues that were camouflaged among the thickets of useless detail. My mind was a master of symbolism, throwing up wonderful metaphors that illuminated the client's inner world. Of course, these skills did not remain hemmed within the boundaries of my practice. They leaked into every part of my life, governing how I thought about myself and the world. "Now I'm expected to give all that away and completely rewire my mind," I thought. "Good luck with that."

At the same time, there was no denying the logic of what my unconscious was saying. Why retire as a psychotherapist just to go on being a therapist everywhere but the clinic. "Alright," I thought, "I'll give it a go. No deeper meanings, no metaphor, no nothing. Just myself and the world."

The challenge came almost immediately in the shape of an old man. He did not introduce himself, or even say hello. In a thick accent that I judged to be central European, he asked what I did. One advantage of a career in psychotherapy is you get used to odd behaviour. I calmly told him my vocation.

"You must know of Isaak Brodsky, The Interpretation of Cakes, and Cake-analysis," he said.

"You mean Sigmund Freud, The Interpretation of Dreams, and psychoanalysis." I laughed, indicating I understood we were mucking around.

"Isaak Brodsky was a patisserie owner in the Pest Jewish quarter early last century," he said, not bothering to hide his contempt. "He understood there was no such thing as a simple cake purchase. You buy the pastry that reveals who you are, at the deepest level. Customers are dying to be understood. But shop owners refuse to do their job." The old man shook his head, as if he could not believe he had to explain this to me. "Bloody Australians! A backward people lacking curiosity! Go to Budapest and find out for yourself." He stormed off.

I tried to dismiss him as a fool, or some poor fellow dementing. If Isaak Brodsky did exist, he was obviously a charlatan, or a rank amateur playing with forces he did not understand. The cake shop could never supersede the clinic. "No one goes to their local patisserie seeking psychological extras," I joked. However, the psychotherapist in me had been triggered. I started thinking about the cakes of my life, analysing how they had shaped me.

I grew up eating typical 1960s Anglo-Australian working class fare: Lamingtons, Cream Buns, and Vanilla Slices. The only expansive cake eating was at Christmas when my Scottish grandmother baked delicious Fruit Cakes, elaborately flavoured with brandy, and topped with a rich marzipan icing. She also made Christmas Puddings, littered with threepenny coins that the finder kept. It was a culinary treasure hunt, adding excitement to each bite, especially for us kids. I now realised granny's Christmas Cakes and Puddings never changed, year after year. Then back to the same old pastries.

One morning, I was watching a cruise ship making its way under the Harbour Bridge, taking passengers off to see the world, when I thought, "There was a message in those cakes. 'Don't expect too much. Work hard and be grateful for what you get.' (In some countries, they can't afford Lamingtons, my mother would have said.)" I suddenly hated those cakes. They represented the narrow-minded, inward-looking Australia of the 1960s.

I wondered if I had found my way into Isaak Brodsky's world. If I had bought a Cream Bun, would he have said, "This cake represents your anger at your upbringing. You have spent your life running from your history and your rage. The cake tells you it's time to face it." Then what would have happened? Would I have just walked out of his shop, armed with my new self-awareness? Or would we schedule further purchases, so I could go deeper into my psyche?

At the same time, my existential issue was painfully apparent. Analysing the cakes of my childhood had helped me understand the arc of my life—I had been driven by a desperate need to escape the dull predictable cake shop of my early years and get to a patisserie that was stocked with endless possibility. However, to get that insight, I had been drawn into psychoanalytic thinking. Not only had I done exactly what my unconscious was telling me not to, I had made the situation worse. Now, not even the cake shop was safe. In fact, I felt a strong urge to head off to the nearest patisserie and buy a cake. If the seller was too lazy to interpret my purchase, I would do it myself.

I did want to follow the path my unconscious had mapped out for me. Not only was I worried about upsetting it, and paying a terrible price for non-compliance, I liked where it was offering to take me. It would be such a luxury to simply accept the world, and myself, at face value. I felt like I was being let off the hook.

I told myself I first needed a break. Then I would set to rewiring my mind. I decided it would be fun to go to Budapest and research Isaak Brodsky and The Interpretation of Cakes. I also thought it would be good to live in a world of different pastries. Given they were not part of my history, they may not trigger associations. Maybe I could just enjoy them for what they were.

I walked out of Budapest's Keleti Railway Station and immediately realised this was not a city that could be taken at face value. Sydney is founded on its stunning harbour. Budapest is built from the unconscious. There are cafés protected by gargoyles, residential entrances bounded by columns crowned with sculpted heads, and walls decorated with paintings of pretty maids gathering flowers. If there was a place where an everyday activity, like purchasing a cake, could inspire psychoanalytic thinking, this was it. "Oh well," I thought, "I'm here now. I'll find out what I can about Isaak. I'll then go home and recode my brain."

I decided not to spend long hours in libraries searching for source materials. I visited the cafés and synagogues of the old Jewish quarter and asked anyone I met about The Interpretation of Cakes. I did not care that no one knew what I was talking about. I was sure word would get around and eventually reach the right people.

After two weeks of stuffing myself with pastries, I was ready to branch out. The fifth Congress of the International Psychoanalytical Association was held in 1918 at The Hungarian Academy of Sciences. I approached the woman on the front desk and said, "It's amazing to think that Isaak Brodsky was offering Cake-analysis around the same time Freud was giving a paper in this building. Imagine Freud buying a cake from Isaak. What would he choose and what would be Isaak's interpretation? It might have changed the course of history." She looked at me as if I was mad. I was getting used to that.

I wandered to Széchenyi István tér, the park that borders the Academy, and sat on a bench next to the Danube. The Chain Bridge was slightly to my left. From my perch, I could see one of the four lion statues that guard the entrances to the span. A little further to the left, on the other side of the river, the Buda Castle sat squat and square on the escarpment that rises above the Danube.

I always found the Palace disappointing. There were no towers or turrets that give a castle personality. That morning, I wondered whether Hungarians were more expressive with their cakes than their buildings. I was considering what that might say about the national character, when an old woman sat down and told me everything she knew about Isaak Brodsky and Cake-analysis. It was not much, but it gave me enough to work with. At least she explained that everything started with Yaakov—Isaak's father—suffering his breakdown. Once you have a beginning, the rest is relatively easy. I thought I would rewrite the story of The Interpretation of Cakes, then go back to Australia.

Each day, I took my laptop to Liszt Ferenc tér. I would sit next to the statue of the great composer, his hair flying as he hammered away at an imaginary piano. I asked Liszt if he had any advice. He said, "Write as if the computer is not there. It's the hardware that gets in the road." I did that, and what follows is my recreation of the story of The Interpretation of Cakes.

Before going on, I first want to apologise to Hungarian readers. I have written the story as an Australian. In the short time I was in Budapest, I did not pick up the Hungarian vernacular.

I would have also liked to write in the style of Mihály Vörösmarty, the great Hungarian dramatist and poet. That would be a better fit for a tale that I believe should be treated as an epic. However, I am a psychotherapist, and that is the lens through which I view the story.

By the time I left Budapest, I was smitten by Isaak Brodsky, this young man who battled in that oddest of places, the intersection between cakes and the unconscious. In an important way, he was a genuine psychotherapist—always a little out of his depth, continually one step behind the truth, and able to land one foot on solid earth while the other hung precariously in space. He kept pushing forward with the naïve optimism that is crucial to psychotherapeutic success. For some mad reason, like any true professional, he believed he would get there in the end.

The shops in Sydney now sell cakes that mirror my country's transition from its British past. The pastries are Continental, Middle Eastern and Asian. You have to work hard to find the simple fare of my childhood. However, the ideas that Isaak struggled with have not been developed. Cake purchasing still suffers from the same minimalism. Want a cake, buy a cake, eat a cake, repeat. No one battles for more.

This work is dedicated to both Isaak Brodsky and that old Hungarian man who accosted me on the banks of the Parramatta River. I wonder if he spent the rest of his life hounding people, or if I was lucky to meet him on a bad day.

AT
Sydney,
2023

1🎂 Yaakov Brodsky's Breakdown

Every cake shop sits in the centre of a powerful tension. On one side is the owner's personality—which ultimately finds expression in the cakes he chooses to sell. On the other, are the expectations of the surrounding social environment.

Some communities see cakes as part of an unbroken heritage. They take comfort in consuming the same pastries their grandparents ate—and in the expectation that their grandchildren's preference will be the same. We can imagine a flashy baker setting up shop in this part of town. A specials board is given pride of place in the store. On it are three different cakes, each described in loving detail, all a combination of flavours and textures that only our creative cake person could imagine.

A fantasy sits in the centre of the shop owner's mind. A crowd of customers stand wide-eyed in the middle of the patisserie. They look at each other and shake their heads. This frisson spreads through the neighbourhood. People discuss topics that were previously prohibited. They read more widely. They shed tears of gratitude for the baker.

This cake man will fail before the year is out. He will be derided as a progressive who contemptuously looks down on his customers, and turns children against their parents. Rocks will be thrown through his windows. His shop will be covered in graffiti.

Then there are the communities where the residents wallow in a cake eating rut. They may not be able to put words to their nagging feelings of disappointment, but they slowly turn away from pastries and consume more sweets and ice cream. A cake man who enters this market expecting to take golfing days, leaving staff to manage the store, is in for a shock. Old favourites will deteriorate on the shelves while his bank account, and his swing, suffer.

A successful patisserie owner is more likely to be a highly intuitive person who is tuned into their neighbourhood, rather than a great baker.

Selling cakes in the Pest Jewish Quarter at the beginning of last century demanded even higher levels of sensitivity. The area was populated by refugees from the pogroms in Poland and Ukraine in the second half of the nineteenth century. When these desperate people reached the Hungarian capital, they made one of history's great collective unconscious decisions. There were no debates or brainstorming sessions. Charismatic leaders did not exhort them to take charge of their lives. Everything happened in the depths of the psyche, where the boundaries between folk dissolve. Highly traumatised people, wedded together by their appalling history, are peculiarly open to unspoken communications. One person thinks, "I hear your thoughts and know you are right." The other nods their appreciation. Down in the depths of their souls, the residents determined they had not escaped oppression simply to waste their lives on petty issues.

At breakfast each morning, the immigrants exclaimed, "Yesterday's coffee was beyond perfection. Today's is even better!" They smelt the flowers in Klauzál tér, the largest park in the quarter. They said, "This scent is so beautiful, it floods the body with joy. One more sniff before I go." They were filling themselves with good experiences they could draw on throughout the day. If they found themselves in an argument that could quickly escalate, they thought, "There are too many good things in life to be bothered with such trivialities."

The inhabitants sometimes woke in the middle of the night, disturbed by terrible images of violence. However, overall, they had collectively repressed these horrors and created an aura of peace and harmony. The Pest Jewish area was known as, "The quarter of a thousand smiles." It was only to be expected that purchasing a cake at Brodsky's Fine Cakes and Biscuits should add to this bonhomie.

For reasons that I have not been able to ascertain—but will comment on at the end of this chapter—Yaakov Brodsky, the owner and manager of the patisserie, could not be the man the community needed him to be. Making matters worse, he had no idea what he was doing wrong. He raved about his morning coffee. "Turkish or Italian? For the life of me, I cannot remember. It does not matter. It was wonderful. What spectacular cake can I offer you."

To some degree, every exclamation of happiness in the quarter was a defence against trauma. Yaakov just seemed particularly fake. His smile sat uneasily on his face. When he told his customers it was a pleasure to serve them, his tone suggested he would rather be somewhere else.

In most places, spending time with an inauthentic baker is no big deal. In the Pest Jewish quarter, it threatened to reveal the community's happiness was only skin deep. Customers stayed away from Brodsky's as a matter of self-preservation. Still, ironically, it was Yaakov's falseness that kept him in business for twenty-four years. Not even the most committed resident could always be happy. Everybody lived with the fear they might groan forlornly in their sleep, startling their spouse with the depths of their despair. Brodsky's was a sanctuary where they could drop their guard.

The customers were not actually conscious that they needed time out. No one walked up to the counter and said, "You're a lifesaver. It's a relief to be with someone who's obviously faking it." They made their purchase, then hovered in the middle of the store, slowly ingesting their cake. Finally, they said, "Oh well, back to the grind."

A few years before the fateful day when he fled from the shop, Yaakov started to sense that something was wrong. Rising anti-Semitism challenged the quarter's positivity. The dawning realisation that the country might lose the War made everyone nervous. More people sought shelter in Brodsky's. They stayed longer and ate more pastries. Eventually, a customer broke down and said, "I can't do it anymore. I'm not happy. I'm scared. You're the only one who knows it's bullshit." The patrons quietly placed their partly eaten pastries on the counter and left.

We can imagine Yaakov's distress at that moment. Not only had he lost his business, but he suddenly had to confront who he was. He had wanted to create a patisserie he was proud of. Instead, his business success had been founded on his failure.

At first, Yaakov managed to stay calm as he stood behind the counter in an empty shop—knowing the veil had been ripped away and his incompetence could no longer protect him. However, over the following days, he started to panic. Unable to stand still, he threw himself into obsessively baking cakes, then stuffing them onto the shelves. Each time he finished one batch, he immediately started another. As he worked, he chanted, "Every cake must have its place. Every cake must have its place. Every cake must have its place."

Yaakov Brodsky fought hard for his sanity. Each time he felt the urge to bake, he told himself, "Yaakov! Be strong! Don't do it!" His words had no effect. He was soon striding to the kitchen. When he reached the baking room, he grabbed each side of the entrance and held tight. His muscles ached. One by one, his fingers lost their purchase. He was then at the mixing table. "Do not blend the ingredients!" "Do not open the oven!" He lost the battle at every stage of the process.

The shelves in the display window at the front of the shop were soon stuffed with pastries. In desperation, Yaakov doubled the number of tiers, radically reducing the space between them. As every cake must have its place, Yaakov determinedly shoved each pastry onto a row. The tops and bottoms of the bigger tortes were severed and flopped onto the floor. Pastries were rammed into the slightest gaps. Cream cakes smudged their neighbours. Cakes with hard surfaces left deep impressions on their softer partners.

Yaakov built tiers along the side walls that went from floor to ceiling. When these sills were filled, he considered erecting a shelving island in the middle of the shop. It would work if customers entered one at a time and passed the stand side on.

After five days of fighting the inevitable, Yaakov finally realised there was no way he could stay in the shop and manage his fear. He decided he would make a little study in the walk-in pantry in the Brodsky flat, and spend his time reading the Torah. Every cake should have its place was a metaphor for every person finding where they belong. He wanted to find his place with God.

I sometimes imagine seeing Yaakov in my practice. As we know, he saw himself as a failure who had to run for his life. However, for reasons that will become evident as we make our way through this story, I would suggest that the pain he suffered was so intense that he could not meet the demand to be positive without turning against himself. Yaakov's breakdown could be seen as an act of courage—a refusal to deny his own distress, that could be why his collapse unleashed the creative energy that gave birth to The Interpretation of Cakes. It was one of the things I loved about my job—the exploration of failure, and its creative possibilities.

2 🎂 The Preparation of a Cake-analyst

Isaak Brodsky was terrified as he walked into the shop the day after his father had fled to the pantry. One reason for his fear was he was only twenty-one years old and had never done a day's work in his life. However, what really frightened him, was the sheer number of cakes. They had him hemmed in. There was no escape.

You could argue it was his father's madness that triggered Isaak's panic. It is deeply unsettling to walk into the centre of someone's insanity, even when they have left the scene. Or, you could say that a pocket of instability had always sat in the depths of Isaak's unconscious. That made him particularly prone to being affected by other people's psychosis. In a way, it really does not matter. What is important is that Isaak's fear quickly escalated and he started to suffer frightening fantasies. The cakes were sick of being sacrificed for instant gratification. They were going to jump off the shelves, push him to the floor and bend him to their wills. He could give over, or get out of their shop.

Isaak knew the pastries were just lumps of flour and cream. They could be as rebellious as they liked, but would end up eaten or thrown in the garbage. This understanding brought no relief. His overwhelmed brain could not say, "Just take a deep breath. Everything will be alright." He definitely could not think, "I'm projecting my fear and anger onto the pastries. It's the responsibility of running the shop that frightens me. I'm the one who wants to revolt!"

We are talking about a young man in 1916, long before a great tsunami swept through our culture, causing everybody to psychologize about everything. Back then, no one said, "Don't put that on me. It's your stuff. Own it!" No one wondered, "What am I seeing in this painting? Do I want to be my own starry night, a sparkling light in the darkness of the world?

Should I be like van Gogh and risk madness in the pursuit of my creativity? Life's hard. Will I ever get a handle on it?" Nevertheless, even by the standards of the time, Isaak was particularly out of touch with his emotions.

I like to think that Isaak's unconscious weighed up the risks that day. He could not go on living as an emotionally stilted human being, and it was time to take a chance. Isaak's psyche let him slide down further into his terrors. It let him imagine the cakes were getting closer. They were about to pounce, and would suffocate him under their sheer weight of numbers. Isaak's instincts were gambling that on verge of losing his mind, he would find the strength to save himself. Thankfully, Isaak was up to the challenge. Out of the depths of his brain, or possibly the darkest regions of his gut, came a scream. He yelled at the cakes, "Take it, you brutes. The shop is yours! Do what you want with it! And to me, too!"

Isaak looked around the shop. The pastries were now sitting calmly on the shelves. He stood quietly for a moment, stunned by the magnitude of his achievement. He then had his first ever reflective thought. "I sit quietly as people talk about me, even when I'm in the room. Now, no predator is safe from my submission." He then shouted again, "Come on! Show your faces. Let me yell my surrender at you. Cowards!" Isaak laughed. "Goodness. This is big stuff."

Isaak then spoke quietly to the cakes. "I know this sounds mad, but I could never have done it without you. You knew I had it in me to throw myself at your feet. You may not get the shop, but I'm certainly yours!" He took another moment to savour what he had accomplished. "Not bad," he said into a shop that now seemed alive with possibility. "Not everyone could do that."

Isaak walked to the display window. He was drawn to the Dobos Torte, but changed his mind and took the Punch Cake. He placed it on the counter and looked at it with brotherly love. "I might scoff you down in one big bite," he said to the pastry. "Just for a bit of fun." Isaak was too new to the world to know that psychological victories never come easy. He had no idea that battle lines were being drawn in the depths of his psyche.

On one side was Isaak's rational brain. Like intellects all over the world, it wanted things to remain as they had always been. It did not care that Isaak's life was severely limited. What mattered was there were no crazy thoughts, intense feelings, or mad behaviours, and he never embarrassed himself or his family. Isaak's rational mind was not against emotional development and personal growth. It just had to be based on scientific principles and guaranteed to work. Spontaneously screaming did not fit the bill. Up until that morning, Isaak's intellect simply had to get him through each day. It now had to stop him from running amok.

Isaak's rational mind knew it could not reassert its authority while he was swept up in the excitement of the morning. While it waited for him to settle, it honed one of its most effective weapons. It strung together the words it would use to humiliate him. "Think you're a big boy, eh. Managed to scream in a shop. What a champion. Soon you'll be out on the street, scaring cats and dogs. Just don't frighten the children."

On the other side was Isaak's unconscious. It had spent the past twenty-one years banished to the deepest reaches of his brain. It was finally getting its chance.

Isaak's unconscious was like every other human psyche. Its one goal was to make him psychologically bigger. In fact, if it had its way, it would make him larger than anyone could possibly imagine. Isaak's psyche thrived on emotional chaos. It did its best work when everything was turned upside down. It had no idea how things would play out, or where they would end up. It was just sure that he would be better for the journey. Of course, as far as the psyche was concerned, the events of the morning had proved the efficacy of how it went about its job. An instance of terror had been turned into a moment of growth. The unconscious looked around Isaak's mind and saw little bits of him that had previously not existed. "Not bad," it thought.

At the same time, Isaak's intuition knew if the rational mind succeeded in humiliating him, he would flee down an internal rabbit hole and never come out. The instincts had to make him even bigger, strong enough to survive the coming attack. They did not have much time.

Before going on, I have to confess to not being a neutral reporter of the coming events. I love the intuition, and how it battles in the face of overwhelming odds. Having said that, I would not be an unconscious for quids. I would sit in my clinic and almost hear the psyche pleading, "I spend my life searching for cracks so I can get my person out of the rut they're in and be more of themselves. All that, after I've been up all night creating wonderfully intricate dreams that will probably be forgotten by morning. And I'm the one they get angry with! At the first sign of emotional pain, they run to the intellect and plead, 'Get me out of here, I'm dying.' Bloody sooks! And what does the great rational mind say? 'Let's go on a diet.' 'We'll get up early and exercise.' 'Let's think positive thoughts.' The intellect! What an amateur!" There are some very angry psyches out there. Not furious at the neglectful mother. Or the father who beat them. But at those weak egos that won't have a go.

We can think of a psychotherapy patient as someone whose life has been thrown into turmoil, but their rational minds refuse to let the unconscious do its job. They need help to wean themselves off their intellect, and learn to trust their instincts. One reason psychotherapy takes so long is the intellect's claws are sharp and deeply embedded in soft flesh. Another is that no one really likes chaos. Patients tend to be scared they won't get through to the other side. They're frightened they will be in pain forever.

Of course, there was no possibility of Isaak getting psychotherapeutic help. His unconscious was on its own and had to find a way to protect him. It had one advantage—for the intellect to be successful, it had to completely dominate Isaak's head, crowding out everything but the insults.

Isaak's intuition decided to play to its strength. It weaved a fascinating daydream, founded on an intriguing narrative, told through a compelling metaphor. The hope was to buy enough time for the world to again intervene, and create another moment of emotional chaos. The psyche would then exploit the situation, helping Isaak to discover another untapped strength within himself.

We would consider this a long shot with little possibility for success. For the unconscious, it's just another day at the office. It plays these odds all the time. That is why it sometimes gives up on gentle prodding and pulls out the sledgehammer and bashes its person into hopelessness and despair.

To understand what Isaak's instincts did, we first need some background information. We can then sit back and watch a genius at work.

The signing of the Austro-Hungarian Compromise in 1867 crowned Hungary's rapid rise from central European backwater to head of an empire. It was a classic rags to riches tale of a nation pulling itself up by the bootstraps and claiming its place on the world stage. One minute Budapest was a dusty village in the middle of nowhere. The next it was a thriving metropolis.

The problem was that rapid industrialisation and increased military might did not automatically lead to international respect. The French and Austrians looked down their noses. "Philistines playing dress-ups" was a typical jibe.

Hungarians chose an interesting way to prove they were more than cultural peacocks. As a nation, they devised a strategy we will call, "Greatness Through Cakes." Anyone with an oven threw themselves into creating sensational pastries. Over three hundred individual recipes were invented during the golden age of Hungarian baking.

The ploy was a stunning success. Hungarians stood in front of their favourite cake shop and said, "Take that you Austrian and French dilettantes. Call us backward!" A new phrase was heard on the streets of Budapest. "We bake. We look the world in the eye."

There was a downside to loading cakes with such a heavy burden. With so much at stake, the free and easy Hungarian pastry industry became serious business. Cafés were now quiet places where pastries were eaten earnestly, as if national pride hung on every bite. Kitchens fell silent as chefs laboured under the weight of responsibility. A popular joke was, "Where are all the bakers who do not reach the Hungarian standard? Out of work, or in Paris."

There was only one socially acceptable exception to this demand for baking gravitas. Mothers were allowed to humour their young charges with cupcakes covered with colourful icing. They could also delight them with sponges shaped like a heart or a puppy. Childhood was now defined as, "The time before serious cake eating."

There was an inevitable reaction to this demand for brutal conformity. Isaak's unconscious transported him to the Kozma utca Cemetery, where an old man stood on a prominent mausoleum. A chef's toque blanche sat on his head and he wore the cook's white apron. In front of him stood a group of twenty bakers. In the way of dreams and fantasies, Isaak knew this was the monthly meeting of the baking anarchists, a secret group committed to challenging the orthodoxy. Their most rebellious act was their creation of the Punch Cake—a gaudy slice of pink jellyroll sponge, topped with a slither of raspberry jam and crowned with garish pink icing—that stood in stark contrast to the usual browns, blacks and whites of Hungarian pastries. They also invented the Marzipan Cake, mocking the Hungarian obsession with the layer cake. The pastry consisted of five tiers of sponge, each separated by green marzipan filling. To make sure the irony was not missed, the cake was topped with a green marzipan icing. "Let them get their tiny minds around that little beauty," they said.

"Comrades," the old man said in a voice that trembled with rage. "Hungarian baking has lost its way. Form has replaced creativity. Experimentation has been sacrificed to the crippling God of excellence. Ask a young chef what he achieved today. 'Sir,' he will tell you, 'I shaved a block of chocolate into perfectly cylindrical caraques. Then I delicately placed each tube on a Poppy Seed and Chocolate Torte, creating a pattern that would have pleased the old masters.' If you asked, 'And did you imagine doing something different?' he would look at you as if you were mad. Our young are being transformed into machines for the reproduction of perfect reproductions. They are the living dead of the dead kitchen." The elder paused, letting his gaze sweep over the cemetery.

"Hungarian baking shapes who we are as a nation. It makes us great. But if cake making is sacrificed to some stiff ideal, we become a sterile nation of boring people, living in a rigid society. Dead cooks, dead cakes, dead people. It's the profound Hungarian equation that will be the death of our country."

Isaak did not decipher the coded message in the fantasy—for all its inflated self-belief, all the rational mind can ultimately offer is stifling predictability. Still, he was sufficiently stirred to yell, "Yes! Dead cakes, dead people! The pastries must be kept alive."

We can now see why Isaak's unconscious led him to the Punch Cake. It was stirring his inner defiance, readying him for the fight with the rational mind. It was also encouraging him to be free and have fun. However, the intellect was lurking. Isaak's psyche still needed that moment of chaos. Fortunately, Hershko Kubrinszky walked through the door. He was an old man, but was about to purchase the first cake of his life.

3 🎂 The First Cake-analytic Patient

Hershko Kubrinszky was born in the industrial suburb of Angyalföld, five kilometres upstream from downtown Pest. Every breath he took was contaminated with the toxins that spewed from surrounding factories. Each spring, the flooding Danube inundated his house, depositing a load of viruses. Hershko was still a boy when he found a job at the shipbuilding yards on Óbuda Island, in the middle of the Danube, near Angyalföld. The docks seethed with disaffected men who managed their shame by humiliating others.

We could imagine Hershko growing into an anxious fellow, constantly jumping at shadows. However, when he was very young and his mind was still being moulded, an ancient instinct told Hershko that a timid man could not survive in Angyalföld. The message was loud and clear—it was his anger that would get him through. Little Hershko swooned as the rage flowed through his body. It crowded out his anxiety and gave him hope.

Of course, Hershko was too young to understand the internal contract he had unwittingly signed. His life would now be a constant battle where he would have to win at all cost. Any sign of weakness would lead to unbearable feelings of humiliation. There could be no room for compassion, especially for himself. He would discover how to hate, but never to love.

Hershko was still a young boy when he learnt to strut around as if he was the king of the world, looking at everyone with contempt. Still, it was eighteen years before he became a fully fledged angry man. For all that time, he kept a secret that he did not even reveal to himself. He was afraid that exploding with rage would blow his cover, leaving him looking impotent and pathetic.

The shift came as a big bully of a man sneered at him. "You don't belong here," the tormentor jeered. "Better run back to mummy." Previously,

Hershko would have relied on bravado. "Fuck you," he would have said, then stalked away, trying to maintain his dignity. Now, he thought, "I could have this fellow for breakfast." Hershko did not say anything, but the tyrant felt his strength, as if it was emanating out of his body. He slunk away, hoping Hershko would leave him alone.

Hershko was tempted to stalk the man and tell him he was the one who should run back to mummy. However, he felt oddly relaxed. An unfamiliar warmth spread through his body. He was happy to enjoy these new sensations. He would wait and launch his rage on his own terms.

For years, an old ship had been decaying at the Óbuda Island Docks. Each morning, the owner slowly walked along the wharves until he was standing in front of the vessel. The fellow would remove his hat, bow his head, and speak quietly to himself. He'd then gaze at the craft for a few moments, before slowly moving away.

If Hershko did not live in a dog-eat-dog world, he might have asked the man what he was doing. Instead, he became irritated that the owner just waltzed into his world, as if he owned the place. He imagined bailing him up and screaming obscenities.

At first, when Hershko fantasised about yelling at the owner, he saw himself shrieking the same abuse he had suffered. The man was a nuisance who got under everyone's feet. He should just piss off and get out of the road. In time, Hershko discovered his own insults. "Your head's stuck so far up your arse you can't see your boat's falling to pieces." "You're a pig of a man who plays games while we work ourselves to death." Hershko was pleased with his creativity. He was developing his own mind with his own thoughts. The day after he realised the bullies could no longer intimidate him, he strode over to the owner.

The sensation of untethered rage was new to Hershko. He could tear the man in two, then destroy his boat. He would then rampage through the docks. Nothing could stop him. "I'm going to smash you so hard it won't be your boat that's falling apart," he screamed. "It'll be you." He spoke with such force he covered the owner in spit.

The owner had spent his life on the docks and was used to the rage of men. The spittle did not bother him. He had suffered worse. He also knew that Hershko would soon run out of insults. Angry men were always hopelessly limited.

When Hershko stopped shouting, the owner quietly explained the boat belonged to his late father. It was now a monument to his father's commitment to creating a better life for the family. Each day, he came to give thanks for his sacrifices.

The possibility of a father sacrificing himself for his family, and a son feeling undying love, touched Hershko. He nearly took the owner's hand and told him he was a good man who would make his father proud.

Some patients would talk about a snake that rose up inside them whenever they felt warm toward someone. The reptile would hiss at the other person, scaring them away. It would then turn and threaten the patient, making sure they did not do anything silly. I see a boa constrictor wrapping its coils around Hershko and wrenching him back from the precipice. "Your father was a fool," he said. "A weak man. Like you. Sink the boat and get on with your life."

The owner had watched Hershko's face soften and experienced a rare feeling of hope. If this man could change, there might be a chance for all the bullies who terrorised the docks. A sweet gentleness could spread through the city. Óbuda Island might be the birthplace of a new world.

Something broke in the owner as Hershko retreated back to his old hardness. He said, "I've been denying it all my life and I just can't do it anymore. My father was like you. A self-centred, compassionless man. He sacrificed nothing. His success was just for him. It made him feel like a big man. I hate to admit it, but I visit this boat every day because it's the only thing he loved. Take it. Do what you want with it. I'm tired of deluding myself."

In Hershko's literal world, he could not conceive that the owner was in the throes of emotional turmoil and might change his mind when he calmed down. "Um, thanks. That's very kind of you," he said, with genuine appreciation.

Theoretically, it might have been possible for a gentle person to survive the rage-filled streets of Angyalföld, and the twisted culture of Óbuda Island, where a day's success was measured by the number of people you humiliated. Hershko was a long way short of having that capability. A green mamba slithered out of the jungle of his mind. "You're an idiot," he said. "I'll be the most famous skipper that ever worked this river."

If there was any chance of the owner changing his mind and keeping the ship, it died with that comment. He did not want to be around these men any longer. "You'll do well," he said.

Hershko Kubrinszky set about recruiting men who were exactly like him—angry fellows who could not bear the humiliation of crewing a failing ship. He knew exactly how to shame them into action. "We'll fail and you'll have to face your wife and kids," he'd sneer. "Imagine how they'll look at you when they're hungry and thrown onto the streets."

It was this skill that enabled Hershko to turn a small profit, shipping goods along the Danube. It could have led to him living a relatively comfortable life. However, each day, he heard the previous owner laughing at him. "Not so easy to become a legend, eh? Not quite the man you thought you were." The shame was intolerable. He had to do something, or go under, psychologically.

Each winter, a weather system called the Siberian High forms around Lake Baikal, in Eastern Russia. Strong weather systems usually keep the high in check. However, periodically, it breaks free and freezes the Continent. Transportation routes become impassable. Lazy viruses that cause the odd runny nose suddenly turn into mass killers. In 1875, the Danube froze from the Black Sea to Passau. Belgrade was isolated, its citizens sick and starving. After the river thawed, Hershko filled his boat with supplies and made a run for the city.

The people of Belgrade refused to pay Hershko's exorbitant charges. He yelled, "You and your children can die! I'm heading to Bucharest. "They laughed at him, "You'll drown in the Iron Gates!" He yelled back "I'm Hershko Kubrinszky. Fuck the Iron Gates!" He pushed on to Romania.

The Danube is a big river, even when not in flood, and the Iron Gates is a dangerously narrow gorge at the southern tip of the Carpathian Mountains. Hershko responded in the only way he knew how. He shamed his men, telling them they were worthless and deserved to die. They got the boat through.

Back in Budapest, Hershko was the hero who had defeated the combined might of the Danube and the Siberian High. Rich merchants now saw him as the man who would get their goods to their destination on time, and above water. Hershko purchased more ships. His charges skyrocketed. He left Angyalföld and moved to the upmarket Castle District, on the Buda side of the Danube. What Hershko did not realise was that he was walking headlong into a powerful shame that would change his life.

New patients would present with anger issues, or tell me they found it impossible to maintain a relationship. They never said, "I really don't like who I am. I want to be a different person." However, for many clients, it soon became apparent it was their shame that motivated them to change.

There is an obvious reason why shame has a bad rap. It is such a powerful feeling, a blunt instrument that tends to be emotionally crippling. It makes sense that people would prefer to see themselves as being pretty much together—with just a few issues that need tidying up. The pity is that this not only means the patient's true motivation for seeking help is hidden, it slows down the process. Once people face their shame, and explore its origins, they tend to let themselves off the hook and become psychologically expansive. They can become a new person.

As we know, Hershko Kubrinszky had no capacity to tell himself that he had done well, and should be proud. Instead, as he walked around the Castle District, his inner voice said, "Who do you think you are, pretending you belong here. Getting through the Iron Gates by throwing the world's biggest tantrum does not make you sophisticated. These people are laughing at you."

We have already seen how the inner contract Hershko made as a small child meant any weakness would lead to intense feelings of humiliation. He felt himself shrinking as he walked around his new neighbourhood. He might have fled back to Angyalföld if he could have survived the shame of defeat.

It was only to be expected that Hershko would respond as he always did. He angrily fought back, throwing himself into challenge of becoming a Castle District man. He found a tailor and demanded that he make him the finest suits. He attended the opera and forced himself to become immersed in the music. He had grown up in a house decorated with gaping cracks and yellow-green mould. He now plastered every wall of his apartment with the works of the Hungarian artist, Jacob Bogdany.

Hershko thought he was just doing what rich people do. It did not occur to him that while he was changing his outer appearance, his psyche was taking the opportunity to radically transform his inner world. He even remained oblivious to what his instincts were up to when he started humming Liszt's rhapsodies, before heading off to insult his employees. He managed to stay naïve when he dropped into an unfamiliar feeling of calm as he looked at Bogdany's, "Poultry and other Birds in the Garden of a Mansion," or "Bread, Oysters, a Chianti Flask, a Lobster, Lemons, and Glasses in a Porcelain Bowl on a Table". However, bit by bit, the green mamba was becoming less lethal. A gentler aspect was growing inside of him, waiting for its chance to strike.

The day before he participated in the first ever Cake-analysis, Hershko decided he needed another painting. The gallery owner showed him Bogdany's "Flamingo and Other Birds in a Landscape". The picture had none of the pastoral warmth of the artist's other works. An oversized flamingo, almost as large as the surrounding trees, was towering over a smaller bird. The flamingo's neck was shaped like a snake ready to strike. There was a reptilian violence in its eyes. The other bird was slightly turned away, as if it knew what was coming. Hershko's unconscious decided the time had come. He told the dealer, "No thank you. I'm sick of being the flamingo. I'm tired of stalking round the swamp, frightening the other birds." Both Hershko and the gallery owner stared at each other. They both knew that Hershko had just made a life-changing declaration, one that had come from his gut.

The following day, as he walked to the Great Synagogue in Pest, Hershko did not bowl along with his shoulders back and his chest out. He let his shoulders slump and his body stoop. He thought it made him more approachable. On the way, he nodded at people and even tried a few greetings.

An hour later, Hershko had reached the Rumbach shul, just up the road from the Brodsky shop. He was ready to try a smile. The next person he met was an old man. Hershko gave him an enormous grin.

Hershko had spent so much of his life scowling, he had to battle against facial muscles that seemed frozen into place. His grin looked more like a grimace. The old fellow must have understood Hershko was doing his best and beamed back. Hershko's next problem was he had never learnt the rhythm of the quarter's smile.

The communal pressure to be positive meant that people were constantly engaged in pleasant salutations. The sheer number of greetings necessitated a grin that was short and swift. Both parties moved quickly to a massive smile, then concluded with a quick nod. Hershko had no idea what to do and kept grinning at maximum capacity. The old man's face became fixed in a tortured smile, while his eyes flickered with confusion. He finally reached out and gently pushed Hershko in the chest. He said, 'You go now.'

Previously, Hershko would have yelled, "Push me in the chest, will you! Come back and I'll show you what a real push is." He now thought, "The old man was just being kind."

Hershko liked the person he was becoming. At the same time, he felt lost in a new world. He could not spend the whole day locked in exaggerated grins and being pushed in the chest. However, he did not want to insult anyone by giving them an inadequate smile.

Needing to catch up with himself, Hershko leant against the wall of the Rumbach Synagogue. Propped up against the shul, he thought, "I battled my way out of Angyalföld, just to end up being pushed in the chest by an old man." He was stunned. About the same time Isaak Brodsky was screaming his surrender to the cakes, Hershko had his first ever revelation. Whenever something irritated him, he would think, "I battled my way out of Angyalföld." "I battled my way out of Angyalföld, just to fight these lazy workers." "I battled my way out of Angyalföld, just to put up with these stupid clients." "I battled my way out of Angyalföld, and still have to fight this ugly river." "I battled my way out of Angyalföld, but no one gives a shit." "I battled my way out of Angyalföld, and will still struggle for the rest of my life." "My God," Hershko thought, "I battled my way out of Angyalföld, just to complain that I battled my way out of Angyalföld. I never actually left Angyalföld."

Hershko felt lighter. Something powerful that had secretly controlled his life had been exposed. A chant started up in his mind. "I battled my way out of Angyalföld. I battled my way out of Angyalföld. I battled my way out of Angyalföld." He tried different pitches. Sometimes high, sometimes low. "I battled my way out of Angyalföld. I battled my way out of Angyalföld. I battled my way out of Angyalföld." He experimented with various tempos. "I battled my way out of Angyalföld. I battled my way out of Angyalföld." An image of rain falling on a ploughed field came into his mind. Suddenly, the meadow was covered in flowers. Hershko called the scene, "Roses, Lilies, Tulips, Marigolds, Daisies, Pansies, Lavender in a Field in Heavy Rain". He felt like crying. He said, "I have battled my way of Angyalföld and I'm going to celebrate with a Dobos Torte." He suddenly found himself laughing.

Hershko did not stop to reflect on why he had decided to buy a Dobos Torte. He did not even know the story behind the cake. Of course, his unconscious knew exactly what it was doing.

József's Dobos opened his patisserie on the upmarket Kecskeméti utca in the 1880s. These were the times before refrigeration and butter was preserved by adding salt. One day, an apprentice accidently used sugar. Most chefs would have fired him immediately. József believed things happened for a reason and every crisis was an opportunity. He thrust his finger into the butter and raised it to his lips. "Magnificent," he exclaimed. "This little delight has been under our noses for centuries. But it took a clumsy boy to bring it to our attention. I'll christen it buttercream."

Hershko's intuition wanted to consolidate the lesson that weakness did not have to evoke crippling shame. Not knowing the pattern of the quarter's smile was the beginning of his discovering how to get out of Angyalföld. As Hershko entered Brodsky's his psyche was ready to crown a good day's work. There would be great celebration as Hershko ate his Dobos Torte.

4 🎂 The Great War

You may remember that Isaak Brodsky was originally drawn to the Dobos Torte. He then changed his mind and chose the Punch Cake. The reason for this was that Isaak's psyche was focussed on the second part of the József Dobos story.

French and Austrian superiority had already been shaken by the new recipes streaming out of Hungary. It was only to be expected that they would push back against József's new discovery. "Buttercream is an interesting, if somewhat frivolous addition," was the dismissive assessment from Versailles. However, when Franz Joseph 1, Emperor of Austria and King of Hungary, tasted the Dobos Torte at the National General Exhibition of Budapest in 1885, his Austrian arrogance collapsed. He said, "I'd go to war over this cake. But with this cake, we'll never need to go to war. The world will be ours. Or Hungary's maybe."

József noted Franz Joseph's confusion and knew exactly what to do. He explored ways to keep his Torte fresh on long journeys to customers across the Continent. He sealed the sides of his cake with nuts and dried fruits. He designed airtight boxes. József told his employees, "With every cake, the world's becoming more Hungarian. The Austro-Hungarian Empire will soon lose the Austro." He was met with loud cheers.

We can see that for Isaak's psyche, at least in that moment, the Torte did not represent how weakness can spur creativity. Rather, it symbolised how spontaneous inspiration could be dragged into the battle for national pride, and subsumed into stifling orthodoxy. It epitomised everything the baking anarchists of Kozma utca Cemetery were rebelling against. It threatened to drag Isaak into oppressive conformity, just as he had screamed his way to freedom.

Theoretically, it would have been possible for these two newly liberated instincts to work in harmony—Isaak with his Punch Cake and Hershko with his Dobos Torte. They could have supercharged each other's growth. Together, they might have invented a metaphorical third cake, or even a new patisserie filled with their stunning creations. Isaak's unconscious was not prepared to take the risk. It did not matter how important the Dobos Torte was for Hershko Kubrinszky. It had to go. Isaak's psyche did something fascinating.

As a psychotherapist, I would sit in a reflective space, listening to the patient, while letting myself experience what it is like to be with them—I could feel sad, angry, oddly disengaged, or any one of a number of emotions. In that contemplative mode, I would make links between what the patient is saying, what they have said in the past, what is known of their history, and what I am feeling. I could watch every step I took as I worked toward an interpretation.

Every now and then, something would cut across that process. Suddenly, my mind was filled with words that seemed to come from nowhere. Somehow, despite having no idea as to their origin, I knew these thoughts were exactly what I needed to say. I would speak with the utmost certainty. In fact, there were times when I would be given only the first few lines. The rest would come after I started speaking. Whenever this happened, the patient would look at me as if I was brilliant. I would feel humble, as if I was being complimented for something that had nothing to do with me. I was even tempted to tell them I had no idea what was going on. The more times this happened, the more I came to trust the efficacy of these insights, and the more they came to me.

There was a major difference between the intervention Isaak was about to make and what I have just described. The words that formed in me were creative—they moved the therapy forward. Isaak's words were defensive—they existed only to thwart Hershko Kubrinszky's unconscious. Still, what intrigues me is how Isaak's psyche took over his brain and had him sprouting words that seemed to come out of nowhere.

Isaak said, "Mr Kubrinszky, for you, the Dobos Torte would be a backward step. You must have a Punch Cake. You might think I'm suggesting that pastry because you are an angry man who wants to hit people. However, the Punch challenges the seriousness of Hungarian baking. You have to eat it because you need to have more fun." Isaak could not believe what he had just said. He stood silently, awaiting his fate.

Hershko's psyche had fought hard that day. It had won some impressive victories, and claimed a considerable amount of territory in his mind. However, it knew it could not win this battle. It just had to let him go back to being the same angry man he had always been, and re-engage the fight later. "Fun, eh," Hershko sneered. "Fuck that for a joke." He smashed the cake and stormed out.

We can imagine the relief in Isaak's unconscious at that moment. It had again chanced its arm and everything had gone perfectly. If Hershko had aimed his rage directly at him, rather than the pastry, Isaak would have withdrawn into himself, never to be coaxed out. Also, if Hershko had thanked him for the Punch Cake, Isaak would not have enjoyed the frisson of upsetting an angry man. What was most important, Isaak's rational mind knew there was no chance of humiliating him at that moment. It slunk away to the back of his head.

5 ♜ Keila Davidovitis Wets Herself

Isaak's unconscious deserved to lay back in a dopamine bliss after Hershko Kubrinszky had stormed out of the shop. It should have been free to replay the events of the morning, revelling in how it had negotiated every challenge. However, an effective unconscious seems to release a pheromone that attracts people desperate for psychological change. Strangers would tell me their difficulties, even when I had not disclosed my profession.

There is a school of thought that says you can read a person's emotions through their body. A bad back shows they are burdened by hefty problems. Skinny people blaze with an anger that burns calories. Obese folk are weighed down by despair. Personally, I think these are prejudicial generalisations that do more harm than good. Having said that, Keila Davidovitis's sadness did sit heavily in her stomach, and dragged her cheeks into hefty jowls. She was the first to pick up the scent emanating from Brodsky's. She bustled into the shop.

Keila wasted no time with pleasantries. "You seem very pleased with yourself," she said to Isaak. "At the same time, you seem a little sad. I've always thought it was one or the other. How do you manage to be both?"

There is nothing quite like the confidence of a psyche that has just done good work. You can imagine Isaak's unconscious laying back in the middle of a couch, its arms spread along the top of the lounge, a self-satisfied smile on its face. It looks at Keila Davidovitis and likes that she is quirky—a perfect foil to Hershko Kubrinszky tantrums.

"Now you mention it," Isaak said, not the least perturbed by Keila's odd behaviour, "I do feel a bit sad. All those silent years when I could have been shouting my surrender. If only the cakes had been there for me long ago. But that grief's out on the edges. Right now, I feel strong, and light as a feather."

Keila Davidovitis did not mind that she had no idea what Isaak was talking about. They were in a dance, working out how to relate to each other. "I used to stand outside this shop when your father was in charge," Keila said. "I'd watch customers go in looking completely exhausted. Is there anything more tiring than having to be happy? Ten minutes later, they'd come out smiling. Your father was a magician. I was tempted to come in myself. But my difficulties run deeper than just staying positive. Café Noé, a small coffee shop on Wesselényi utca, was a better fit for me. I always ordered a Flódni."

In one respect, the Flódni sits neatly in the Hungarian baking style. It is a layer cake consisting of five tiers, each separated by a filling. However, where most layer cakes are based on the sponge, giving them a generous look, the Flódni is founded on small strips of sweet pastry. It is one of Hungary's few compact cakes. Rather than a simple cream, or even József Dobos's buttercream, the Flódni has four different fillings: poppy seed, apple, walnut and strawberry jam. The Flódni is the thinking person's layer cake.

Some Flódnis are made with mathematical precision, each stratum cut perfectly, with no filling leaking out the sides. They reminded me of a soldier standing at attention, everything rigidly in place. Café Noé's Flódnis were roughly made with the filling spilling out. They seemed on the verge of falling over.

"'This cake is just like me,' I'd say to the waitress at Café Noé," Keila continued. 'On the edge of collapse. Still, the smallness of this café helps me feel safe. There's not enough room to fall, physically or psychologically.' That girl was old beyond her years. She never responded as if I were mad.

"I sat at the rear of the Café where my back fitted perfectly into a cavity in the stone wall. I'd pull the top layer off my Flódni and slowly devour it. I'd then move to the next. As I worked through each level, I felt I was going deeper into myself. My husband, Berko, died ten years ago and I believed if I could touch my grief, I would finally be free of my pain. 'It's here, somewhere,' I'd tell myself as I ate each layer. 'A flood of tears waiting to well up and set me free.' Of course, the Flódni couldn't save me. I just didn't know what else to do.

"Then, a few days back, I noticed your father madly forcing cakes onto the shelves. As I watched, I realised I'd never seen anyone lose their mind, then fight their way back. No one had ever shown me how it was done. I knew I was clutching at straws, but Yaakov might be my man.

"The point came when your father had stacked so many cakes in the window, I couldn't see inside. I managed to contain myself, even when I heard him making new ledges. Everything then went silent and I had to find out what was going on. 'I understand,' I said to Yaakov, as I looked around the pastries. 'The stone walls at Noé's stopped me from falling. I now need a soft place. The darkness makes it even more gentle. This is where I'll cry.'

It did not occur to me that your father had created his own refuge and I was interrupting him. He started chanting, 'Every cake must have its place, every cake must have its place, every cake must have its place.' He rushed to the baking room. I was elated. The deeper he went into his madness, the greater the chance he could help me."

Keila realised she was talking to a young man about his father. He had every right to march her out the door. Her psyche had to act quickly. The tactic it chose was to push words out of her mouth, like bullets from a machine gun. Keila's statements did not have to make sense. They just had to overwhelm Isaak, stopping him from feeling disgust.

"I hurried down to Café Noé and told the waitress, 'Brodsky's has been turned into a giant pastry womb. It'll be the place of my rebirth. I just need to wait until that poor man works his way out of his darkness, and can show me how to get out of mine.' She said, 'I hope he makes it. For you, and the world.'

"This morning, I saw a pastry had been removed from that mass of cakes in the window. I expected to find your father, a man who no longer needed a sealed womb and had taken his first step back to sanity. I found you, somehow completely born and ready to go." Keila then noticed the squashed Punch Cake. "Looks like someone was not happy with their pastry."

"I told an angry old man to buy that cake rather than a Dobos Torte. I said he needed to have more fun."

"What made you do that?"

"The cakes spoke through me."

Keila's strategy had worked. She was safe. "Why are they not speaking through you now? To me?"

"I don't know. But there's something in my head that doesn't seem very useful."

"Tell me what it is."

"Alright. But don't blame me for wasting your time."

"I promise."

"I completely understand why the anarchists at the Kozma utca Cemetery want to challenge the seriousness of Hungarian baking. But the Punch Cake is too gaudy. It's more a parody of itself and the baking radicals than Hungarian cooking. All it proves is that pastries should never be used as political statements. They should bury it out at the Kozma utca Cemetery, in the failed pastries section." Isaak shook his head. "My mind used to be dead. Now I blurt out these crazy things."

"What do you think of the Chocolate Chestnut Roulade?"

Keila was referring to the cake that reached the Hungarian court of King Matthias after he married Princess Beatrice, daughter of the king of Naples, in the late fifteenth century. After his first bite, the cheeky Matthias exclaimed, "Darling, I thought I only wanted to eat you."

The root of roulade is the French word "rouler", meaning to roll. To make a Chocolate Chestnut Roulade, you first moisten a flat jelly roll sponge—flavoured with chocolate, coffee, dark rum and chestnuts—with butter, for easy rolling. A rum flavoured cream filling is spread over the sponge, which is rolled into the shape of a log and cut into sections. The Brodsky's added blanched almonds for an unexpected bite.

"I think it's a very good cake that deserves to stay above ground," Isaak said.

"You've missed the point. The Roulade is popular in the quarter because it's founded on a fundamental deception. It tastes good, it looks presentable, but it represents a life that goes round in circles. The Roulade is about being stuck while pretending you're happy. I ate dozens of them before I realised what was going on." Keila smiled. "I know I'm in the right place. My mind is suddenly alive."

Before that morning, Isaak did not have enough sense of self to be offended. He now felt something precious was being taken from him. He said, "Mrs Davidovitis. It's not up to you to reveal the meaning of the Chocolate Chestnut Roulade. Your job is to come into the shop and choose a cake. The pastry then talks through me. In fact, the pastries might suggest another cake altogether. You may have wanted to take this pastry womb off my father, but this cake thing is mine."

Keila knew there was no going back to Café Noé. The ritualistic eating of the Flódni that had held her together for ten years would now feel hollow. She had to keep Isaak on side, or slip into a depression from which she might never recover. "My dear boy," she said. "Your poor father could not find himself in this patisserie and had to run for his life. You've only been here a few hours and already you're saying clever things about the Punch Cake. I have no intention of taking it from you. I know very well what it means to lose something of value. We'll do this together."

Tears welled in Isaak's eyes. "Thank you," he said. "I thought it would be just me and the cakes. It never occurred to me that someone might help. No one's offered in the past."

Keila Davidovitis started to cry. Big tears rolled down her cheeks. Suddenly, she wet herself. An odorous stream of urine spread across the floor. Isaak made to run around the counter to comfort her, but Keila put up a hand to stop him. "You generously accepted my offer to work together, even after I had offended you with my thoughts about the Chocolate Hazelnut Roulade. You cannot believe how deeply that touched me. Well, obviously you can see it. I knew I needed to cry but the tears wouldn't come. Maybe I had to pee out the pain as well." Keila lifted her dress and proudly examined her effort. "I suspect this sort of thing happens all the time."

"Um, no. I don't think anyone's peed in the shop before."

Keila's rational mind seized the moment. "Pissing yourself in public! The boy makes it very clear you're the only one who has ever done this. Bet that makes you feel good about yourself."

This time, Keila's psyche landed on a novel strategy. It confused the rational mind by mimicking its own love of precision. Slowly and clearly, without a metaphor in sight, she laid out exactly what she wanted. "I know I suggested we work together. However, I now need you to quietly listen to what I have to say. I hate ordering you around, but I have no option. I trust you can go along with me."

Fortunately for Keila, and the future of The Interpretation of Cakes, Isaak was deeply moved that someone would take him seriously enough to ask him to take them seriously. "It would be an honour," he said. "I'll do my best."

I know I am biased, but there is nothing more beautiful than a person reaching out and receiving a caring response. You could imagine someone telling Keila she did not need anyone to listen to her. She was a strong woman who could look after herself. Is there anything worse than evading your own rational mind, only to run headlong into someone else's? It takes a special person to patiently listen to someone standing in a pool of urine.

Isaak's generosity brought more tears from Keila. She lifted her dress to check for further signs of leakage. Her bladder held firm. "Looks like I wee when I'm sad, but not when I'm feeling gratitude. That's interesting."

"I might just stick to the cakes, Mrs Davidovitis. I'll leave the urination stuff to you."

Keila smiled. "I wonder what my life would have been like if I peed in a cake shop ten years ago. I could have confidently left my mark all over the place, if you get my drift. Every shop owner would scramble for their mop as I burst—excuse the pun—through their door. I'd better get on with my story."

"Yes, I'm new at this listening thing. Best not test me too much."

"Berko saw himself as both a man of his time, and ahead of his time," Keila continued. "He said, 'I have one foot in the past, one in the present and one in the future.' He believed he was a comedian as well as an intellectual.

"Berko insisted the only place a free thinker could take coffee and cake was the Auguszt Café, over in Kossuth Lojos utca. 'A liberal cake shop, for the liberated mind,' he'd say.

"You probably know the Auguszt. Doesn't matter if you don't. What's important is it fits neatly into classic Budapest café design. It has a large front window, high ceilings, chandeliers and marble topped tables. However, rather than being decorated with paintings by Hungary's finest, on one wall is a drawing of a huge bird that looks like an overgrown turkey, ridden by a man. On the other, a large elephant is the centre of a parade. It's surrounded by scantily dressed men playing musical instruments. 'The Auguszt is a fusion of traditional and avant-garde,' Berko would say. 'It takes what it wants and mashes it together. It doesn't give a damn!' He was so clever.

"Berko believed the Auguszt was a place where customers should break out of their gossipy cliques and join in free discussions that involved the whole café. 'It's not enough to carry on about the excellence of the morning coffee,' he'd say. 'It should unleash an avalanche of free association. Coffee takes us to the Ottoman occupation. That leads us to think about the Turks and their love of the bathhouse. We then see ourselves luxuriating in the soothing waters of the Széchenyi Spa, and ponder the importance of warm water to our nation. Without the spa, we'd be like the Austrians, a people with no understanding of sensual pleasure. Imagine a café where those conversations took place.' Berko spoke loudly, hoping someone would join him.

"Given the importance of baking to Hungarians, the idea that a café would create a fusion between classical and modern did not sit well with the people of the city, even if this rebelliousness was confined to drawings on the wall. How could that encourage serious cake eating? Imagine what the Austrians and the French would say. Their contempt would be unbearable."

"This Café is just down the road?"

"Yes."

"Then why didn't all this stuff happen there? Cakes being smashed, women peeing on the floor?

"Great question. But your job is to listen. Anyway, I expect you'll soon get your answer.

"Patrons of the Auguszt Café were derided as, 'The mad turkeys of the mad turkey.' It took courage just to walk through the door. Joining in crazy conversations with a loud mouth was a step too far. Never mind smashing cakes and weeing on the floor. You have to come here for that!" Keila laughed. "The other customers went on with their discussions, ignoring the silly old man. 'It's like the Turks stole our tongues,' Berko complained. 'We'll move to Paris where people talk freely.'

"Then, ten years ago, he called out, 'Our Parliament Building is basically a series of arches and spires, all reaching up to the sky. It looks more like a church than a legislature. Hungary doesn't know whether to be ruled by Man or God.' No one responded and he lowered his head in defeat.

"'It should look like a synagogue,' I said.

"Berko was shocked. He never expected it would be his wife who'd join him in his crimes of free association. 'Make parliament a shul,' he laughed. 'That would be Rabbi rousing.' Sorry. I expect it's the curse of the intellectual to tell terrible jokes that only they think are funny. He kissed my forehead, and whispered, 'I'm not alone.'

"'You never were.'

"For the first time ever, Berko and I were on the same level. I should have been happy to leave it at that. But I couldn't stop myself.

"Margit Island lies upstream from the centre of the city. Stop me if you know any of what I'm telling you. I want you to listen, not be bored."

"It's best to assume I know nothing."

"Alright. The island used to be the hunting playground of the Hungarian Royal family and called the Island of Rabbits. It was renamed in honour of Saint Margit, the daughter of Béla IV, King of Hungary. The King made a pact with God; cast out the Mongols and he would commit his daughter to a lifetime of service in the nunnery he would build on the island. God must have had nothing else to do that day. The heathens left Hungary immediately and Margit moved to her new home. God must have been distracted when the Ottomans later destroyed the island's beautiful churches and monasteries."

"I didn't know that."

"What you may know is that like most Danube islands, Margit is shaped like a tear drop. 'I understand the island was moulded by the sediment load of the river,' I said to Berko, 'but I like to think it was fashioned by Margit's tears. She was upset at being a bargaining tool, even with God. All those wonderful trees were watered by her crying.' I thought it was a lovely image, but Berko eyes filled with tears. 'Poor Margit,' he said. 'There's no escape.' It had started so well but was quickly going downhill.

"'I'm with you,' I pleaded. 'Margit has brought us together. We can sit here every day and analyse the city. Tomorrow, the Buda Castle. The day after, the Great Synagogue. Margit truly is God's little girl. You can't change the world, Berko. You can't even change the Auguszt Café. But you've expanded my mind. Can't that be enough? If everybody helped just one person, imagine where we'd be.' What I said was true. I was a different woman because of him.

"'No. It will never happen,' he said.

"I realised Berko was not creating a beautiful island as he cried for the human condition. His tears were for himself. Not only was his wife cleverer than he believed, she might be more intelligent than him. 'Berko doesn't want me to be a mad turkey,' I thought. 'There can only be one mad turkey and it's him.' I only understood my place in the relationship when I stepped out of it.

"Berko never recovered from the distress at losing his position. He died a few days later. It was bad enough losing him physically. Seeing him as the ultimate Chocolate Chestnut Roulade was devastating. He was trapped in the endless circle of his own self-belief.

"I wished I'd let Parliament House be Christian and left Margit to cry alone. Berko and I would still be together. He'd be the mad turkey, while I'd be the little wife sitting in awe at his feet. That's alright. There are worse lives. I decided never to be intelligent again.

"Now I'm standing in a pool of wee and have never felt better. My bladder is empty and my mind is full. I'm talking like a woman who knows what I'm talking about. I'm the maddest turkey."

Isaak also felt good. With Hershko Kubrinszky, he had learnt to let the cakes speak through him. With Mrs Davidovitis, he was discovering how to listen. "I'll get the mop and clean up."

"You don't need to do that. You listened to me. You let me be clever again. You've already cleaned up enough." Keila gave a smile that was ten years in the making.

Isaak felt something was not right. He heard his father chanting, "Every cake should have its place. Every cake should have its place." Keila Davidovitis had been given her place. If she stayed longer, she would have taken too much attention and something would be lost. Isaak pretended to sweep her out the door. "The hardest part is still to come," he said.

Neither Isaak Brodsky nor Keila Davidovitis understood the warning— Keila had started to reclaim herself in the shop and it would not be easy to walk away. Still, deep within herself, Keila sensed it was time to depart. "I know what you mean," she said, and headed off.

Keila not only resolved her grief that morning, she also lost her self-consciousness. As she walked to Café Noé, she tested the quarter's positivity by proclaiming, "I smell better than the flowers at Klauzál tér."

As Keila sat in her usual seat at the back of Noé's, she realised she no longer needed the stone walls to hold her. In fact, the Café felt spacious, as if there was plenty of room for this bigger version of herself. She pulled off the first layer of her Flódni, then thought, "I don't need to do this anymore." She finished the cake in a couple of bites. "That's the best pastry I've ever eaten," she told the waitress.

Meanwhile, as Isaak Brodsky mopped up Mrs Davidovitis's wee, he again thought, "Every cake should have its place. Every cake should have its place." The words carried none of his father's obsessiveness. Nor did they convey the firmness that heralded it was time for Keila to go. They were soft, like the quiet expression of a simple truth. Isaak had started the day as an empty hole in the fabric of the world. He was now finding his place. He looked at the disappearing puddle. "It would be good to get there without having to piss in public," he thought. "Still, if that's what it takes, then that's what it takes."

Isaak Brodsky had almost reached the point of no return. An important shift was happening inside him that was propelling him toward a career as a Cake-analysist. Soon, he would have no option but to devote his life to The Interpretation of Cakes. Let me explain.

I would spend years battling away with my patients, trying to crack an issue that affected their lives. Then, without any forewarning, the smallest of threads would come loose. It would be incredibly subtle, but we both knew the world had shifted. It's a moment of closeness, even intimacy, between two people that's rare in this world. The deepening of the relationship creates a longing for more. Sure enough, the next issue comes along and the hard work begins again. We would go round this circle many times before the patient was ready to leave. It sounds addictive, but it's basically the same mechanism that creates affection between parents and children, intimate partners, or groups engaged in creative endeavours. That's why psychotherapy is so powerful.

By the time I was nearing the end of my career, I started to wonder what it meant to spend every day of your working life in this dynamic. Do you become someone who sees emotional pain as the first step toward a warm feeling and a closer connection? Would that encourage you to fight on in difficult relationships? Would you lose the capacity to throw up your hands in defeat and leave?

These questions where all in the future for Isaak. After Hershko Kubrinszky smashed the Punch Cake and thundered out of the shop, he was happy for the day to end. After Keila Davidovitis, he was feeling that psychotherapeutic warmth and was desperate for more. You could feel him being drawn into the gaping maw of the Cake-analytic world. As tends to be the way of these things, he had just put his mop away when he got his wish. An eighteen-year-old woman walked through the door.

6 ♟ Goosebumps

Aliza Lövy walked to the counter and said, "Mr Brodsky, I need you to calmly spend time with me, and get me out of here as swiftly as possible. I know I'm asking the impossible, but that's how it must be."

"You don't want me to listen to your story?"

"No."

"If you choose a cake, you'll learn something about yourself. You might even discover you've picked the wrong pastry."

"I know who I am and what I want. Can we just get on with it?"

Most psychotherapy patients enter the process expecting the therapist to do whatever psychotherapists do. What they do not understand is that they cannot just sit back and let the practitioner guide them down a well-worn path. They have to create the therapist they need. It is the job of the client to force the practitioner to grow, so the therapist can help them to grow. At one level, a therapy is ultimately two people pushing the other to confront their limitations, while helping each other to work through them. If either party does not commit to this process, the therapy will fail.

Isaak Brodsky had enjoyed being moulded by Hershko Kubrinszky and remoulded by Keila Davidovitis. However, he was too inexperienced to realise that Aliza was offering him another chance to grow as a Cake-analyst. He pushed back. "Miss Lövy," he said, "I've finally found my place. Please respect that."

"Mr Brodsky, I'm a member of the Kazinczy Synagogue, the quarter's Orthodox shul. If I'm found alone with a man, I'm dead. I'm not interested in you and your so-called place."

As we know, Isaak's unconscious had been focussed on warding off the inevitable attack from his intellect. It had not expected a strike from the outside world. Isaak was unprotected. His brain began to freeze.

This time, Isaak did not scream his surrender, as he had on that first morning when he entered the store. His psyche decided he would stay stony silent. Meanwhile, it flooded his head with anger. "How dare you come into my shop and tell me what I can and cannot do," Isaak thought. "Who do you think you are?" It did not matter that he did not speak these words, Isaak's mind was alive.

Aliza was completely oblivious to what was happening inside Isaak. She said, "The other girls say they get goosebumps when they're with boys. I've always thought life was about discovering interesting facts and solving complex philosophical issues. Now I want to experience goosebumps. There's a gap in the window that someone could see through. Can you plug it?"

"I'm sorry," said Isaak. "The Punch Cake that filled that spot was smashed by Mr Kubrinszky just before Mrs Davidovitis wet herself."

Aliza had imagined that experiencing goosebumps would be a straightforward procedure. She would be alone with a man and they would burst out all over her. She had not expected to find herself in a place where weird things happened. She felt disorientated and her unconscious took advantage of the situation. It placed an image in her mind. A group of girls were walking past. They all had goosebumps and were laughing excitedly. They did not bother to look at her.

I suspect Aliza's psyche knew she would push back against the feeling of inferiority it had created in her. It was playing the long game, slowly manoeuvring her into position.

As her instincts had predicted, Aliza tried to reassert herself. "The thing is," she said to Isaak, "the Kazinczy is on my side. The actual building, not the congregation. It's sure that goosebumps would be good for me." Aliza realised she was not making sense. She started to feel foolish. She stopped talking.

We can see that this would have been a great opportunity for Isaak's unconscious to teach him about empathy. It could have helped him to sense that Aliza was struggling. It would have got him to say, "It must be wonderful to have the Kazinczy in your corner. It must make you feel very special. Let's get going with those goosebumps." What makes the psyche so endearing is that it always surprises. Isaak's instincts decided this would be his Punch

Cake moment. He said, "What did the Kazinczy say? Smash a cake or wee on my floor?"

Isaak's brazenness hit the mark. "I certainly won't be doing that," Aliza said. "My hands are loose and my bladder is tight."

You can feel how close they were at that moment—two people with their rational minds disabled, and edging each other toward aspects of themselves they had not previously explored. (I would say that they had already met one of the criteria for a successful relationship—they were helping each other to discover themselves.)

What blindsided both participants, and their psyches, was not the sudden attack from Aliza's rational mind, humiliating her for talking about her bladder. The problem was that things were moving too fast. Aliza had suddenly found herself in a place she had not expected, and had not experienced before. Her inner cobra rose to its full height. She said, "I thought I needed a clever man who was well versed in the physiology of goosebumps. All I need is a clod who can smash a Punch Cake."

It goes without saying that Isaak Brodsky had never met anyone like Aliza Lövy—someone who craved intimacy, but was afraid of it. What made things worse was the feeling he had done something wrong, even though he had no idea what that could be. All he could muster was a defensive, "It was Hershko Kubrinszky who smashed the pastry."

"That's not important. What matters is the damn cake—excuse my French—was smashed. Why am I always surrounded by idiots who say stupid things?" She shook her head. "I'll never have goosebumps."

Isaak looked down at the floor. His arms fell loose by his side.

Before that morning, Aliza would not have cared that she had defeated Isaak. He was a fool who had got what he deserved. However, she had enjoyed their joking about smashing cakes and peeing on the floor. She was disappointed that she had ruined it.

Aliza Lövy had never repaired a relationship in her life. Not knowing what to do, she said, "I'm going to tell you a story about the Kazinczy Synagogue. It will help you understand how I came to be standing in front of a man who smashes Punch Cakes."

Isaak started to correct her.

Aliza put up her hand to stop him. "It's not important who smashed the cake," she gently said. "Without you, the pastry would be intact. You destroyed it, whether you actually bashed it or not."

This was a step too far for Isaak. He stood silent.

"As you probably know, most synagogues in Pest, including the Rumbach and the Great Synagogue, are built in the Moorish Revivalist style. They celebrate Medieval Islamic Spain, a time of tolerance when Jews thrived. Those synagogues have minaret-like towers, domed roofs on top of octagonal ceilings, arched entrances and facades built from bricks of different colours, laid to create an audacious pattern.

"The Kazinczy comes from a younger tradition. About thirty years ago, the Viennese elders decided to dismantle the city wall and replace it with a grand boulevard, called the Ringstrasse. They lined it with neo-Classical, neo-Renaissance, neo-Baroque and neo-Gothic buildings. Civic leaders thought they had brought sophistication to the city. More progressive citizens were appalled that the town's great architectural leap forward was a step back to a past that wasn't even Austrian. If Vienna was going to take its place in the modern world, it had to create its own identity. They designed buildings that featured large flat surfaces, decorated with colourful tiles, ceramic motifs, and even painted figures.

As you know, these people called themselves the Viennese Secessionists and the architecture is referred to as art nouveau."

"I'm afraid I know nothing of art nouveau," said Isaak. "Up until this morning, I did not even realise the patrons of the Auguszt Café were called mad turkeys. A whole world has been going on around me without my noticing."

I have no doubt this was the moment Aliza's unconscious had been moving her toward. She was furious that having goosebumps meant standing in a crazy cake shop with a stupid man. It was always like this. Moving out of her head and into her body meant humiliating herself. "Of course, you don't know about art nouveau," she spat at Isaak. "You live in a cake cave!"

This time, Isaak's psyche did not fill his head with rage. Instead, he stood silent. He said nothing because there was nothing to say.

It was in this quietness that Isaak discovered what he needed from Aliza. He wanted her to understand how painful it was to find yourself with a lively person when you have spent your life emotionally numb. She did not have to offer solutions. Nor did he need her compassion. She just had to acknowledge she had come looking for goosebumps from a boy who had just discovered he had a pulse.

The silence also allowed a feeling to rise up in Aliza. She was ashamed that she'd hurt someone who had been kind to her. She said, "I'm sorry. I didn't mean to be cruel. I just know if I leave without getting goosebumps, I'll have missed out on something important. I may never get another chance."

Isaak realised Aliza's apology came from her fear of missing out, rather than remorse at hurting him. He did not mind. He had seen himself clearly. It no longer mattered whether she saw him. He said, "Miss Lövy, please tell me more about the Kazinczy Synagogue."

"I like to think the roots of the Kazinczy can be traced back to the Viennese Secessionists," Aliza said. "Its façade is a large square wall, with absolutely no classical flourishes, like columns or archways. Its beauty lies in its mass of colourfully tiled monuments. Its fascia is topped by a series of colourful ramparts.

"On a corner of the Synagogue, right at the top, are a collection of Stars of David. They're made out of luscious red tiles. Each day, I look up at them and the Kazinczy speaks to me. 'You can push the rules without breaking them,' it says. 'You can be yourself, while staying true to the community. You can be Orthodox and art nouveau. Thrilling, isn't it? You're the only one in the congregation that understands.'

"I watched your father fill the window with so many cakes you couldn't see inside. I've always thought of myself as sensible but a silly idea came into my head. 'That's where I can be alone with a man and have goosebumps.'

"The obvious problem was your father is not young. However, he seemed so troubled I thought he might have to leave. It was madness, but I stood across the road at eight these past mornings to see who opened the shop. Today, it was you. I thought, 'This is my chance.'

"I couldn't come straight away. I first had to ask the Kazinczy whether I was doing the right thing. 'Yes,' it said, 'I'm sure he's a good boy who won't take advantage of you, or shame you for being forward. Cake men carry the burden of Hungarian pride. They can't afford to do anything stupid. Be on your way.' Now, I'm here, covered in goosebumps. Look at my arms!" Aliza lifted a sleeve, then quickly pulled it back into place. "Isaak, may I have a Kréme. Please move quickly."

The Kréme symbolises one of the great tensions in Hungarian baking. It is a simple cake—a slab of vanilla flavoured custard is wedged between two slices of flaky pastry. However, despite its apparent simplicity, the cake is the ultimate test for serious chefs. With the famous chocolate cakes—like the Dodos Torte—mistakes are concealed by the richness of the chocolate. With the Kréme, there is only you, the cake and the custard. There is no hiding a pastry that sticks to the roof of the mouth, or a custard that is lumpy. Baking connoisseurs love the Kréme. The obvious analysis was that Aliza wanted to be the best she could possibly be, but did not want to be metaphorically covered in showy tiles.

Isaak knew all he had to do was speak the interpretation and the cakes would keep bringing him amazing insights. What he said was, "Aliza, you're the perfect Kréme. You'd never stick to the roof of the mouth, nor feel lumpy in the back of the throat."

Aliza blushed. "No one has ever called me the perfect Kréme. You're giving me more goosebumps." She turned to leave.

"Aliza," Isaak called. "You forgot your Kréme!"

"Keep it. It's done its job."

There were times, after an intense day in my clinic, when I looked out my window with wonder at the bigness of the world, and how it brimmed with possibility. I felt larger, my patients had worked me hard, and something had grown within me. After Aliza left the store, Isaak stood silently looking at the cakes. "What an amazing day," he said to the pastries. "And it all started with the stupid Punch Cake. I don't know if the anarchists at the Kozma utca Cemetery will ever change Hungarian baking, but they have certainly turned my world upside down."

Isaak's thoughts turned to his mother and sister waiting upstairs. For the first time in his life, he wondered how their day had gone. He hoped his father had spent a productive day in the pantry and taken a first step out of his madness. He then sat peacefully, waiting out the afternoon until it was time to close the shop. He then walked out the door and up the stairs to the apartment. He was dying to tell his family that he was finally finding his place.

7 🎂 Isaak Brodsky Confronts the Kugelhopf Breast

Isaak was so filled with the noise of the day, he forgot to prepare himself for the suffocating silence of the Brodsky flat. He opened the door and felt the life being sucked out of him. An inner voice yelled, "Run! The loungeroom window! Go!"

Isaak fled past the kitchen and the bedrooms and into the sitting room. He reached the window and took a deep breath. It felt like the last gasp of air in the flat. He heard someone moving behind him and was tempted to turn around. An inner voice said, "Keep looking out. Don't move until we know you're safe."

We already have a good idea why Yaakov was silent. He had spent the past twenty-three years failing to create the cake shop that would make him proud. He could have filled the apartment with endless moaning about how useless he was. He might have wailed that life was unfair and the world picked on him. He could have stomped round the apartment and thrown things across the room. Yaakov was too crushed to complain. He spent his nights looking at the floor, shaking his head and silently asking what went wrong. It was true that he had retreated to the pantry, but the weight of his despair still hung in the air.

Where Yaakov was lost in the silent agitation of defeat, Isaak's mother, Nina, sat in the blissful quiet of a person who needed nothing more from life. Somewhere in the past, she had been picked up by a wave of warm energy that carried her through each day. She was not compelled to say anything in the present as everything had happened in the past. The rest of the family had no idea why Nina was so content. They simply walked past her as she sat in a lounge chair, blissfully smiling.

Isaak's sister, Shoshana, was two years older. She was intelligent, compassionate, sensitive and artistic. She was also a great beauty. When Shoshana Brodsky shook her waist length black hair, it was as if she scattered the night. Her milky white face framed eyes that were as black as the darkest sky. Where Nina was sustained by the events of the past, Shoshana lived in the future, where she hoped her existential problem—how to be chosen when no one could not choose you—would be resolved. She was silent because there was only one thing to say in the present. "This is not it and it's driving me mad."

Still staring out the window, Isaak's gaze was drawn to the two towers of the Great Synagogue, a few hundred yards to the south east. Isaak whispered, "Aliza, the Great Synagogue truly is the best example of Moorish Revivalism in Pest. Islamic Spain was a golden age for Jews, and this is a wonderful time for me."

The Synagogue's columns were crowned by copper orbs and each cupola was decorated by gold trimmings around their equators. The setting sun suddenly caused the gold to flare against the dull background of the globes. Isaak almost broke into tears. "It's like watching myself burst into light in the darkness of the cake cave this morning," he said. "No one in this apartment gets me. They don't even try. Only the towers of the Great Synagogue understand." Isaak wondered if his family had heard. "I don't care," he said a little louder. "At least it means they hear something."

The earth turned, the orbs faded, and Isaak's eye was drawn west to the Royal Palace. The castle had turned pink, as if the sun was both drawing it out of the darkness of the escarpment, and from its own lacklustre self. "Miss Lövy," Isaak said, "Why does the Hungarian Palace look so boring?"

"My dear Mr Brodsky," came Aliza's reply, "the Magyar people were never going to accept a castle that belonged in a fairy tale. That's for the Austrians and the French. They have their heads in the clouds while our feet are planted firmly on the ground."

"Thank you. Is there anything you don't know?"

"Now I've had goosebumps, everything's been cleared up wonderfully."

Isaak turned and was surprised to find his sister sitting on the three-seater couch that faced the window.

Shoshana had not been affected by her father seeking refuge in the pantry, or her mother being roused to take meals to him. Her indifference even survived the preposterous spectacle of Nina baking a cake. However, her brother rushing past her bedroom was too much. She crept silently into the lounge room. A creaking floorboard betrayed her. Isaak stiffened, but did not turn around.

Shoshana had heard Isaak complain that the family did not understand him. She witnessed his strange conversation with Aliza about the Buda Castle. Then, in what was the greatest shock of all, he was now smiling, as if he was pleased to see her.

There had been a time when Shoshana Brodsky had tested the world, pushing and pulling at any possibility that might resolve the riddle of wanting to be chosen, but being too desirable to be freely selected. There were moments when someone did see beyond their own needs and caught a fleeting glimpse of her. They tilted their heads, as if studying a foreign object. Their voices rose an octave at the shock of seeing a person behind the beauty.

Shoshana's problem was that she could not contain herself at those moments. She gushed about the times they would spend together and how they would be close friends. In a sense, Shoshana projected onto these folk what everybody thrust onto her. She lost sight of them as people and saw only what they offered. The person would retreat and Shoshana was left with the pain of having messed up again. She finally gave the game away.

Shoshana was now desperate to ask, "Isaak, what happened to you? How did you suddenly burst into life? Can you show me how it's done?" She managed to keep her agitation in check.

I would love to have had Isaak in my clinic that evening. I would have relished the opportunity to discover why his unconscious kept resisting the chance to teach him compassion. Or, to put it another way, why it was so wedded to the Punch Cake. What I can report is that the memory of asking Aliza if the Kazinczy had told her to smash a cake or wee on his floor suddenly filled Isaak's head.

By now, Isaak was starting to trust his intuition. It helped him navigate the difficult interactions that were constantly confronting him. At the same time, he realised he could not be as disinhibited with his sister as he had been with Aliza. His job was to speak freely, but not too freely. "Shoshana," he said, "did you know the Kazinczy shul can be traced back to a rebellion in Vienna. The building, not the congregation. It all started with the Secessionists."

Shoshana rose to the occasion, as if all she ever wanted was someone to play with. She said, "Are you saying my face is flat and needs prettying up with tiles?"

It was testament to the hard work Isaak's instincts had done that day that he did not retreat. "Don't worry," he said. "You can be Orthodox and art nouveau."

"I suppose you could, but why would you?"

"Because it would give you goosebumps."

"Isaak! What's happened to you? Father used to come home each night more depressed than the last. The shop was killing him. One day in the store and you're talking about goosebumps." She held her breath, concerned she had pushed too hard.

Isaak would not be put off so easily. "Would you smash a Punch Cake if it made you a better person?"

Shoshana laughed, "I would. But to be the best person I could possibly be, I'd destroy an Esterházy Cream Torte."

"You can't do that! The cake was named for a good man!"

"You don't see the value in smashing a good man? I could name a few I'd like to smash. They're not so good around a pretty girl."

The Esterházy Cream Torte is made from a delicate almond flavoured sponge, cut in two, and separated by a filling of whipped cream flavoured with rum and marsala. The cake is topped with almond flavoured whipped cream, sprinkled with confectioner's sugar.

For Cake-analytic purposes, the Torte's symbolism stems from it being named for the cultured Paul III Anton, Prince Esterházy. A privileged member of Hungarian royalty, Anton could easily have chosen a life of physical and spiritual hedonism. Instead, he committed himself to a difficult diplomatic and political career where he often suffered humiliating defeat. The Esterházy Cream Torte exhorts us to not give over to the temptations of sloth or excess, but to meet life's challenges through diligence and hard work.

Isaak was ready to risk everything. "Would you wet yourself in public if it helped you grieve for a husband you lost ten years ago?"

"Well, young brother, the score is very much in my favour. I've left a trail of broken hearts and can keep my ablutions private. Though it might be the reason you see so many drunk men weeing against walls. Try tapping them on the shoulder and ask if they're one of my casualties."

It occurred to Isaak that everything he had said to that moment had been introduced to him by someone else. The next statement had to be his. He said, "Shoshana, I think someone like you needs to live in a city that has a real castle. You know, beautiful towers and turrets. Not one that relies on the setting sun to make it attractive."

Shoshana burst into tears. "Isaak, I know nothing about the Kazinczy shul or the Viennese Secessionists. I've never seen anyone smash a cake or wee in a shop. I've been stuck here, living in a cocoon. Then you walked out of this flat as the quiet little mouse you've always been and came back completely transformed.

"Let me tell you something about goosebumps. Try walking around a city where everybody wants to get inside you. I don't mean physically. They want to inhabit you, so you can never leave them. Every pore in your skin is a flaw in your defence. They got in. They pulsed through my body. I got plenty of goosebumps, but they were never mine. I can't spend my life filled with other people's desires. But there's no way out. If I peed in public, I wouldn't know if it was my wee." She paused to dab her eyes. "I can't tell you how much I've wanted to be a pastry that sticks to the roof of the mouth. I've never felt as lumpy as I did with you just now. We were having fun. Why did you have to get so serious?"

"I needed to say something that was mine."

"Tell me this. When do I get something for me?"

Isaak shook his head. "Mrs Davidovitis was right. Things go downhill so quickly."

"I'm sorry, Isaak. I know you're doing your best. Anyway, mother's coming."

The wave of warm energy that Nina Brodsky had ridden for decades began to ebb that morning. She had no idea why her husband took refuge in the cupboard, but felt compelled to support him. Stirred into action, she then baked a Kugelhopf. She placed the pastry on the coffee table in front of the three-seater couch.

The foundational ingredient of the Kugelhopf is a soft yeast dough, which is mixed with raisins, almonds and cherry brandy. Hungarians often add sweetened ground poppy seeds.

The Kugelhopf is cooked in a bundt baking dish, a large bowl with fluted sides. The most striking feature of the bundt is the outsized "chimney", which rises from the centre of the base. The chimney amplifies the contact between metal and mixture. This facilitates a wider distribution of heat, ensuring the centre cooks at the same rate as the edges. Larger cakes can be baked without burning the extremities, or leaving the middle underdone. The bundt's design produces a pastry that is large and round at the bottom, rising to a pointed apex, with a gaping hole piercing the centre, courtesy of the chimney.

Isaak exploded. "Mother! That cake looks like a big breast! Yesterday, I would have eaten it without thinking. Now I understand the importance of choosing the right cake. That pastry is a backward step. It's worse than a Dobos Torte for Mr Kubrinszky. Take it away. I can't have it near me."

"Thank you," said Nina. "That explains something that was bothering me. While I was baking, I kept remembering your birth. It happened under very bad circumstances and I was not the nurturing mother I would like to have been. Your taking over the shop gives me a second chance to be there for you. I'm going to be the biggest breasted mother that ever lived. From this moment forward, I'm all Kugelhopf."

Isaak nearly burst out crying. He crossed his legs and looked at Shoshana.

"I'm nearly peeing myself as well," she said.

The three Brodskys quietly enjoyed the Kugelhopf. At first, they took turns taking a bite, then peeling off to the toilet to relieve themselves of the grief from years of silence.

Finally, Isaak asked, "Mother, can you explain why you were not there for me?"

"I'd be happy to. But we'll have to wait for the right cake."

"Can you at least tell me how you know about this cake business? The pastries seem to be speaking through you. Like me in the shop."

"I'm sorry, I can't. I just had to bake the Kugelhopf. I didn't realise it was a big breast until your outburst."

"We need more cakes," said Shoshana. "Maybe they'll tell us what's going on around here."

8 ♛ Hershko Kubrinszky Teaches Isaak Brodsky About Anger

Isaak Brodsky was grumpy as he stood behind the counter the following morning. "Why won't mother tell me what happened when I was a baby?" he said into the empty shop. "A Kugelhopf breast doesn't wait till it has sorted out its pastry!"

An hour went by without a customer coming into the store and Isaak turned on the cakes. "Great job with Hershko Kubrinszky, fellas. Not much after that. Nothing when Mrs Davidovitis peed on my floor. Silence as Aliza Lövy strutted round with goosebumps. Seems like you've shut up shop and gone home." The door suddenly opened. Hershko Kubrinszky entered, flashing a wide smile.

Hershko had suffered a devastating attack from his rational mind as he left Brodsky's the previous day. "Such a good man," it sneered. "Bashes a defenceless cake. There's another patisserie up the road. We can go there and you could prove your goodness all over again."

I have struggled to imagine what it would be like for an unconscious to be defeated by another psyche, as happened to Hershko's unconscious in its struggle with Isaak's. I suspect one of the intuition's strengths is it never sees itself as beaten. Or, to put it another way, defeat is its way of life. The instincts are battle-hardened because they are always in the fight.

The rational mind has the opposite problem. It believes it can win the war with one fell swoop. By the time Hershko reached the Chain Bridge, his intellect was ready to drive home its victory. "No more operas," it said smugly. "No Bogdany's."

What the rational mind did not realise was that it had left the door open for Hersko's unconscious. The psyche surreptitiously planted a seemingly innocuous thought in his brain. "It's been a big morning. Let's go for a walk and catch our breath." Hershko wandered quietly along the river until he crossed the bridge to Margit Island and found a bench among the trees. His psyche gave him time to settle, then set about normalising what had happened in Brodsky's. "You smashed a cake. So what? Who hasn't? You haven't lived till you've bashed a pastry."

Another advantage the unconscious has over the rational mind is that its care is authentic. People teach themselves to say things like, "It's alright. You're safe now. Just calm down." It does not work because they know it's fake, they manufactured it themselves. Hershko could feel his psyche was speaking from the heart. He reflected on all the good things that had happened since he had decided he no longer wanted to be a flamingo. He even allowed that there was something funny about an old man thrashing an innocent Punch Cake. He thought, "Isaak Brodsky was the first person to look into my soul. He did not want to take advantage of me. It was a genuine act of kindness. I need to spend more time with him."

As he walked to the counter, Hershko trusted Isaak would notice his smile was not the perfunctory grin of the quarter, but a genuine attempt at reparation.

Isaak was having nothing of it. He snarled, "The pastry killer returns!"

Hershko Kubrinszky automatically settled into combat mode. He observed the slight curve in Isaak's back. Experience told him his legs, hidden behind the counter, would be tense, ready to drive him into the fray. At the same time, Isaak's arms hung loose. "This one's not going to think strategically," Hershko decided. "He'll make a huge lunge, while swinging windmill punches. No neat upper cuts or lethal right hooks."

Hershko used to love sizing up an opponent. His mind felt wonderfully calm while his body buzzed with adrenaline. It was one of the times the two parts of him worked in harmony. It now seemed old and boring.

Isaak's psyche sensed Hershko was backing off. It realised that this was a rare chance to learn about anger with a man who knew all about rage, but was not on his game. Without thinking (or with a considerable amount of inner thought, depending on how you look at it), Isaak said, "So you've come back to bully another Punch Cake. Makes you feel like a big man."

Hershko's unconscious sensed he was barely hanging on. At any moment, he could slip back to being the flamingo that lived only to terrorise the swamp. This time, the psyche did not act like a guerrilla fighter—pulling back, waiting for a better time to attack. Instead, it reached for its bluntest instrument. It shut Hershko down, leaving him standing voiceless in the middle of the shop. With Hershko immobilised, his instincts took him back to when he was a young child. His brother had stolen his bread and was provocatively eating it in front of him. Little Hershko's face burnt with shame. He felt the rage pulsing through his body.

The intuition's hope was that Hershko would realise he was no longer a child that had to win every battle, or be overwhelmed with the humiliation of being weak. He could generously play a part in Isaak's growth as a Cake-analyst, a development that would eventually be good for Hershko as well. He said, "I've come back to tell you why I wanted a Dobos Torte. I need you to listen."

Isaak could not believe his luck. This bully, who had spent his life intimidating everyone, was offering his head on a platter. "Mr Kubrinszky, tell someone who cares."

Hershko was so proud of Isaak, he wanted to take him in his arms and hug him. In this moment of openness, Hershko then had an important insight. "The hug is as much for me as it is for Isaak." Hershko felt good. "This is what it is like to feel affection for someone," he thought. Then, his mood quickly changed. "If I don't hug Isaak immediately," he thought, "the feeling will slip away and I may never get it back. I'll spend the rest of my life as a hollow man, living without love."

Hershko's unconscious decided it was too soon for Hershko to enjoy his hug. There was more work to do. Hershko said, "You think you're strong but you'll always be a Punch Cake. Squashed by the world."

Isaak stormed around the counter. As Hershko predicted, his wild punches hit nothing but air. He quickly wore himself out and was soon bent over with his hands on his knees. "I feel so weak." He began to cry. "I'll never be strong enough for anything."

Hershko finally had the chance to wrap Isaak in an embrace. "You did well," he said, sounding paternal. "You should be pleased with yourself." He then whispered, "You might not understand this, but I'm hugging myself as much as I'm hugging you."

I believe the image of the father who made sacrifices for his children had been lodged in Hershko's mind as he spoke to the owner of the decrepit boat at the Óbuda Island Docks—the fantasy that the owner destroyed by revealing the truth. In fact, I would now say that was the spark that initiated the determination in Hershko to become a better man. It predated his move to the Castle District and his attending the opera and purchasing Bogdany paintings.

As a rule, it is not a good idea for the patient to parent the therapist, or for the practitioner to attempt to punch the client. That would generally be considered to cross a number of professional boundaries. However, Hershko needed Isaak to be the son he'd never had. At that point in his psychological development, it was the only way he could show affection. Despite all the obvious technical and ethical issues, it seemed to work.

Isaak stayed in the old man's embrace until he had no more tears to cry, then he subtly tried to re-establish his position as the Cake-analyst. He said, "You came to tell me why you wanted the Dobos Torte, but ended up having punches thrown at you. That's not fair. Tell me about the Dobos."

Hershko was not ready to go back to being the client. He said, "I think the real reason I came was to make you angry. That was my gift to you."

"You're very kind."

"Thank you. You felt anger. I felt compassion. It doesn't get better than that."

9 ♕ Nina Brodsky Dances at the Medzhybizh Town Hall

A storm hit Budapest the evening after Hershko Kubrinszky had graciously spiked Isaak's anger, enveloping the two towers of the Great Synagogue in a premature darkness. Isaak thought about the column growing inside him. "It's out of sight, but I can feel its presence," he said to himself. He turned to find Shoshana, waiting expectantly on the couch. He said, "Mr Kubrinszky's problem was that he was the angriest person he knew. There was no one to show him how to deal with his rage." He chose his words carefully, not wanting to upset Shoshana. "Your difficulty is you're too beautiful. No one has ever faced the same challenges. There's never been anyone to show you the way. You've retreated to the flat, but that won't work."

"There once was a woman in Liszt Ferenc tér," Shoshana said. "She wasn't as gorgeous as me, but wasn't far behind. She looked defeated. I wondered if it was my beauty that was too much for her. I suspect it was her own."

"I'm the first cake seller to ever work with the mind. I'm not sure I want to be a pioneer, spending my life wandering lost in the wilderness, with no one showing me the way. I'm thinking of getting out."

"I'm sorry, Isaak. But you're in the same position as me and Mr Kubrinszky. You've got to see it through to the end."

"How do you know that?"

"I used to watch how people dealt with my rejection. Some got angry, as if I had no right to deny them. Others seemed suddenly exposed and ashamed. Then there were those who kept chattering away, as if we were talking about the weather. They all had one thing in common. They came to me before they were ready. Some were nearly there. They almost could see me. They just couldn't wait. You're like those people. If you leave the shop now, you'll hurt yourself and others. You'll pay for the rest of your life."

"I don't know what to say."

"Of course, you don't. You need time to work it out. Why do you think I've been sitting here all these years?"

"I hope it won't take that long."

"We'll see. The thing is, I think mother's Kugelhopf was as much for me as it was for you. The big breast got into my head, if you know what I mean, inspiring all these thoughts." Shoshana lowered her voice. "Just between you and me, I'm angry with mother. She should've baked the Kugelhopf years ago."

There's an important question here that needs to be addressed. Cake-analysis had already changed Isaak's life for the better. He had experienced psychotherapeutic warmth, and it was drawing him into the profession. Yet, somehow, he had found the strength to resist. It started when he did not speak the interpretation to Aliza. Now, he was telling Shoshana he wanted to get out. I have given a great deal of thought as to what was happening inside Isaak. I think his unconscious was trying to protect him.

To survive as a psychotherapist, and a Cake-analyst, you have to get plenty of love outside your practice. In fact, you can only safely enjoy that psychotherapeutic warmth if there is enough affection elsewhere in your life. I'm not talking about crossing sexual boundaries, though that is a possibility. I mean not having to rely too heavily on the relationship with your patients, and getting lost in something murky.

As Shoshana had said, Isaak still needed more from Cake-analysis. However, his intuition knew he had to experience a lot more love before he could turn The Interpretation of Cakes into a career. It was trying to walk a fine line—helping Isaak to get enough from Cake-analysis for him to be big enough to survive without it.

Nina entered with three Syrniki and placed them on the coffee table.

Syrniki, or Russian Pancake, is a Ukrainian staple. It was popular during summer, before refrigeration, when milk was likely to turn. Sour milk is heated to cause protein denaturation, then strained to create quark cheese. The quark is added to flour, then the mixture is flattened and fried on a skillet. Syrniki is traditionally topped with Morello cherry preserve and rolled into a tubular shape. These days, cooks tend to use farmer's cheese rather than quark.

"What's this?" said Shoshana. "The little breast?"

All three laughed.

Nina said, "Your father and I are sitting on the front porch of my family's house on the banks of the lake at Medzhybizh, our shtetl in Ukraine. My mother offers us Syrniki."

"Is this the beginning of your explaining why you weren't present when I was a baby?" Isaak asked.

"Yes. And it will help Shoshana understand why she's so beautiful."

"It wasn't just nature?"

"No, love."

Lightning struck nearby, followed by a clap of thunder. Nina waited for silence, then said, "First, you have to know this is not a memory. Yaakov grew up in a rich family and my mother was too embarrassed to have him in our house. She would have died before she served him a basic cake like Syrniki. This image comes from the depths of my soul."

"Is there any other place?" Isaak asked.

"Not when you're talking about cakes," Shoshana replied.

"Medzhybizh was very conservative," Nina continued. "Public displays of physical affection, even between married couples, were frowned upon. Then came the storms of Negev, in the early 1880s. Negev is the Hebrew word for the south, while storms referred to the pogroms. The pogroms of southern Ukraine. The residents became even more reserved. They needed a place to let off steam.

"Medzhybizh sits at the junction of two big rivers, the Southern Bug and the Buzhenka. You can grow anything on the surrounding plains. Given the richness of the area, you'd expect the village to have a grand town hall. The community made a collective decision that the building remain small and simple. No one actually spoke about this. It was as if each individual took the idea into their minds, nodded their approval, and passed it on.

"Whenever there was a wedding or Bar Mitzvah, a curtain was placed down the centre of the dance floor to keep the sexes apart. However, the Rabbi always left early and the curtain was ripped down. Suddenly, men and women were packed tight, dancing together. Drenched in communal sweat, the villagers danced in a warm soup of erotic pleasure. It was an orgy where everyone kept their clothes on, and never touched each other sexually. Still, the most enthusiastic Klezmer band was drowned out by ecstatic groaning.

"Of course, I'd never needed to dance at the town hall. Yaakov loved me to the core of my being. He touched me all over without laying a hand on me.

Shoshana said, "Is it possible to be loved by someone who does not want to consume you?"

"Well, even though your father didn't touch me, he wanted to devour me, if you know what I mean."

Shoshana nodded.

"I'd never thought of myself as beautiful or ugly, skinny or fat. If anyone had asked me to describe myself, I would have told them to speak to Yaakov. He was the one who really saw me.

"I have no idea why everything fell apart on my wedding day. Something inside me decided it was time to step out of Yaakov's shadow. It might be one of life's ironies that when you're ready to couple, you're finally able to be alone."

Shoshana smiled. She liked that thought.

"As my mother and sisters fussed over my hair, I immodestly thought I was as pretty as the rhododendron covered hills in spring. As they made up my face, I decided I was as attractive as the wild cherries reflected in the waters of the lake. Standing in my white dress, I finally accepted I was the prettiest girl in the shtetl. It was the first time I had a sense of myself outside of Yaakov.

"That evening, I lost myself in the beat of the music and the rhythm of the crowd. In that crush of wet bodies, my breasts tingled and my nipples stood erect. I discovered that my pubic area responded to pressure. Sorry, I'm just going where the story takes me. Blame the Syrniki if you must.

"I'd thought the other girls wasted their lives on petty crushes, broken hearts and spiteful jealousies. Saturated with sweat and sexual fervour, I saw it was Yaakov and I who had missed out. We'd believed we lived at the top of the mountain and didn't need anybody. It was an illusion that stopped us from growing as people. We're still paying the price.

"The moaning was so loud it was impossible to isolate one person from another. But Yaakov heard only one thing—my spiralling into a pleasure that didn't include him. I can't honestly apologise for my behaviour that night. We couldn't go on as if we were everything we needed. I'm just sorry it had to be so brutal.

"I suddenly thought I was going to burst. I dashed toward the exit, knowing Yaakov would follow. I raced to my family's house. By the time he arrived, I was standing naked on the veranda, the full moon caressing my flesh. I rushed toward my husband and was about to jump into his arms and wrap my dripping legs round his waist. He raised his hand, signalling me to stop. I almost tumbled into the lake. Yaakov grabbed me. He would have gladly let me drown. He pushed me away and looked at me as if I was the most damnable woman. I stood defiantly nude, my chest combatively forward.

"With a strength neither of us knew he possessed, Yaakov quietly explained life in Medzhybizh was too dangerous. He'd heard of a Jewish quarter in Leopoldstadt, across the canal—whatever that meant—in Vienna. He knew his family wouldn't help us, but he believed he could get us to Budapest.

"I was naïve, but not completely stupid. I knew your father had been shamed by my recklessness and could no longer show his face in the shtetl. But his hiding behind the pogroms confused me. I fell into his arms and said, 'Budapest it is.'

"Yaakov explained that if we were going to start a new life, the last thing we needed was another mouth to feed. We couldn't gamble with sex.

"We confidently strode out of the shtetl but it takes more than a night's dancing in the Medzhybizh Town Hall to become streetwise. If it wasn't for the slither of worldliness I'd gained in the sweaty throng, and the steel Yaakov had forged while angrily watching me, we would never have reached Budapest.

"Our lodgings, when we finally got here, were appalling. I'd cleaned the barn after the cattle had been housed all winter. Nothing prepared me for the stink of the Rákos patak. It takes sewerage from Angyalföld to the Danube. The stench caught in your throat and worked into your flesh. You know the Budapest saying. 'How do you pick an Angyalföldian? Stand downwind.'

"Yaakov dragged himself to the Óbuda Island ship yards. The poor man had lived a pampered life. They laughed at him and he ran away. But that terrible moment for Yaakov changed my life. Without it, I would never have found that warm feeling that sustained me until Yaakov left the shop and Isaak took over."

"It was your buttercream moment," said Isaak, "in the József Dobos sense."

"I see what you mean," said Nina. "These cakes are wonderful things, once you get to understand them."

"Please tell me why I was so dead," Isaak asked.

"You haven't explained why I'm so beautiful," said Shoshana.

Nina picked up a cake and said, "Thank you mother for all those Syrniki." She turned to her children. "We need another pastry before I can answer your questions."

10 ♟ Hershko Kubrinszky's Shame

A disturbing scene haunted Isaak's mind as he stood behind the counter the following morning. His mother was dancing at the Medzhybizh Town Hall. Her head was thrown back. She rubbed her hands over her chest. A hand went lower.

I said earlier that the unconscious has only one goal—it wants to make us bigger. Morality is not its problem. Isaak had to become a sexual being at some point, and his mother had provided the spark. Isaak obviously did not see it that way. He was disgusted with himself.

Isaak's rational mind had spent the last few days sitting at the back of his brain, patiently waiting for the foolish unconscious to do what it always does—take a step too far. It was time to reclaim its ascendency.

The problem for Isaak's intellect was it suffered from the same irredeemable character flaws as rational minds all over the world. It was condescending, unimaginative and predictable. It started with the inevitable reprimand. "See what happens when you let the instincts take charge. It's exciting at the time, but look at the trouble it causes. Calling Aliza the perfect Kréme was creepy. And let's not even start on those conversations with your sister."

If the intellect had stopped there, it might have won the battle. Isaak felt so ashamed, his relationship with his unconscious would have been permanently damaged. However, having put the young upstart in his place, the rational mind could not resist the temptation to prove its mastery. It swept the vision of Nina out of Isaak's head, and replaced it with a benign image of him drinking coffee at the Auguszt Café. It then filled his brain with patter. "The maddest turkey ever. Too mad for words. What's this turkey on about, anyway?" The intellect was sure Isaak would choose these humorous images over the sordid fantasies his unconscious dished up.

The thing was, Isaak began to feel cheated. He had been appalled by the vision of his mother dancing, but he longed for it to come back. This was not some perverse Freudian Oedipal desire. He sensed he was being offered something important that he would never find with the mad turkeys. The image of the Auguszt Café faded. The picture of his mother dancing at the Medzhybizh Town Hall swept back into his head.

Sometimes, in the rare moments I can get past its inflated self-belief, and the devastation it leaves in its wake, I feel sorry for the rational mind. It staggers around with no idea of the complexities it is dealing with. The intellect picked itself up and reran the same strategy. Isaak was now standing outside the Kazinczy shul, looking up at the stars of David. It was telling him he could be Orthodox and art nouveau.

The irony was, if Isaak had been allowed to sit calmly with the image of his mother at the Medzyhbizh Town Hall, he would have realised how badly he wanted to dance with Aliza. They would both be covered with goosebumps. If he then went deeper into himself, he would have discovered his hope that the two of them would live in eternal bliss.

The obvious question is why Isaak's psyche did not simply explain all this to him. Why put him through the discomfort of imagining his mother's disinhibition? The instincts knew something the rational mind would never understand. If everything had been laid out logically, Isaak would have just shrugged his agreement. For him to really get it, down in his gut, the message had to be wrapped in emotional intensity. For some reason, that's how we are as humans. There is no other way.

Of course, Isaak's intellect continued its pathetic challenge. "What about Margit Island?" it said. "All those wonderful trees."

Isaak strode to the display window and grabbed a Kréme. He ran his right index finger through the custard and rubbed it over the back of his left hand. His rational mind was tempted to say, "Parliament House should look like a synagogue," but it knew the battle was over. It slunk away to the little nest it had created at the back of the brain.

With his intellect defeated, Isaak lifted his shirt and massaged the custard onto his stomach and chest. "Beautifully smooth," he thought. He then ran the top layer of pastry around his face. "It might not stick to the roof of the mouth, but it adheres perfectly to the skin."

Isaak Brodsky had never danced in his life, but he managed to swing his hips from side to side as he shuffled around the shop. He held the Kréme in front of him, and said, "You give me goosebumps!" It sounded flat. He wanted sultry. "You give me goosebumps." His self-consciousness forced him to speak too quickly and a little high. That was alright. He was happy with what he had achieved. He had no idea what to do with the Kréme, so he ate it.

I suspect Isaak was now strong enough to withstand a renewed attack from a severely weakened rational mind, even after covering himself in cake. We will never know. Hershko Kubrinszky again came into the store just as Isaak had taken another psychological step.

"You look perplexed," Hershko said as he reached the counter.

With his intellect out of the picture, and nothing between his unconscious and the world, Isaak said, "I feel like the apple filling in the Strudel. All wet and gooey and covered in pastry. Have you ever felt like that?"

"No, I haven't, but looking at your face and hands, you seem more like the custard in the Kréme."

I'm sorry to interrupt the narrative again, but there are things we need to know if we are going to understand what Isaak's unconscious was doing.

Over a thousand years ago, nomads in Central Asia experimented with cutting unleavened dough into very thin slices before baking, thereby reducing the moisture content. Under dry conditions, the bread lasted two years. When needed, it was slightly dampened with water, covered with cloth, then left for about ten minutes to refresh and soften. It became a staple on the great westward journeys along the Silk Road.

Turkish bakers discovered that adding oil enabled them to stretch the dough thinner. The Ottomans then cut it into even smaller pieces, stacked the slices on top of each other, separated by clarified butter, or delicate honeys and nuts. This was the genesis of baklava. The pastries were introduced to Hungary during the Turkish occupation of the sixteenth century. Rather than cutting and layering the dough in the Ottoman style, the central Europeans rolled it into large sheets. They then added a variety of fillings the Turks had never contemplated. After the withdrawal of the Ottomans, Hungary was absorbed into the Austrian sphere and the pastry travelled to Vienna. It was named Strudel, possibly after a large vortex in the Danube, upstream from the capital.

There are the usual arguments as to whether the Austrians, Germans or Hungarians created Apple Strudel. One day, a Cake-analytic academic will decipher why apple's popularity outstripped the sour cherry, poppy seed and the savoury, and why it was as fashionable in the Castle District as in the Angyalföld slums.

What is important for our story is that Isaak's reference to himself as an Apple Strudel symbolised his increasing understanding that he was not solely his own invention. The Strudel grew from the inputs of a variety of folk from different cultures. Even when he was dancing around the shop covered in cake, Isaak was the creation of all the people in his life. He was becoming bigger than he could imagine.

"I was thinking of buying an Esterházy Cream Torte," said Hershko Kubrinszky.

"That's exactly the right pastry. You generously let me take a few swings at you. You're the Anton III of the cake shop."

"I now think the Esterházy is yesterday's pastry. Today, it's the Chimney Cake. You talking about being the apple sauce in the Strudel got me wondering about myself. I used to be filled with anger. I now feel empty."

The Chimney Cake is from Transylvania, then part of the Austro-Hungarian Empire, and therefore claimed by Hungarians as one of their own. A thin ribbon of dough yeast pastry, flavoured with cinnamon, is wrapped round a steel baking cylinder, forming a hollow helix shaped pastry, tapered slightly toward the ends. The pastry is rolled in sugar, and cooked slowly above an open fire while regularly brushed with butter. The sugar caramelises, forming a shiny crisp crust. The butter creates a golden hue. Chimney Cakes are usually sold from temporary stands rolled onto the streets each morning.

One of the things to understand about therapy, is it is not necessarily a problem if the therapist is psychologically messed up. In fact, the last thing a patient needs is someone who has got it all together. How could they possibly understand your struggles? What is important is that the therapist is at least a step ahead of the client.

It was his own recent experience of feeling empty that told Isaak it would not help if he said, "That's not true, Mr Kubrinszky. You're a man filled with life." The platitude would have denied Hershko's reality and signalled that Isaak did not want to feel his pain. The best thing Isaak could have done was empathise with Hershko by acknowledging how confronting it must be to experience himself that way. He then would have waited to see how Hershko reacted.

What Isaak said was, "Mr Kubrinszky, I don't think I can help you today. I've just rubbed a Kréme all over my body and danced around the shop. It's scrambled my mind."

Therapists usually do not disclose these types of things. They try to remain anonymous, allowing the patient to project their inner lives onto them. That is how the practitioner discovers how the client thinks about themself and the world. However, as we have seen, Isaak had developed a unique therapeutic relationship with Hershko. His personal disclosure was immediately effective.

Hershko spoke softly, his voice breaking. "People have always been afraid to reveal themselves to me. They were frightened I'd humiliate them. They were right. In fact, I can feel it now. 'You're obviously a pervert.' 'Can't you find a woman to touch you?' I'm sorry. I don't want to think those horrible things." He then went quiet. "I'm not empty," he said. "I'm filled with shame."

This time, there was no possibility of Isaak avoiding an empathic response. Hershko's shame seemed to rise up from the floorboards and drip down the walls. He said, "You poor man."

Hershko let out a sigh, as if his body had been bracing for an attack. "Thank you."

Even after thirty years of experiencing these moments of mutual openness, I still find them hard to describe. You feel deeply in touch with one another, but also in your own space. It feels infinite, but also complete. You would like to stay forever, but also want to move on.

"When I went through the Iron Gates, I wet myself," said Hershko. "There, it's out."

"That's it!" Isaak was genuinely amazed. "That happens all the time. People wee all over the place." Isaak watched the relief spread across Hershko's face. "I wish I could wet myself. It seems freeing. All I've managed to do is dance around the shop covered in Kréme."

"You have my deepest respect for that."

"And here's another thing. Imagine what sort of man you'd be if you didn't wet yourself at the Iron Gates. You'd have stayed hard, like iron. The weeing rusted the steel in you. It's why you felt you never left Angyalföld. You're the odd man out in the Castle District, a place where men lack the courage to wet themselves."

"It's true. Those businessmen are pissing themselves with fear, and too afraid to piss themselves."

"There's a real downside with the way Hungary built pride through cakes. All those people sitting in cafés, acting like they're special, simply because they eat the best pastries in the world. They think the Chimney Cake is beneath them. But that's the real Hungarian pastry. An empty cake for an empty nation."

"Thank you. You've changed my life." Hershko reached over the counter and took Isaak by the shoulders. He said, "I'm sorry, but I won't be coming back. It's time for me to join the mad turkeys at the Auguszt Café. You'll have to stay and help the next old man who thinks he needs a Dobos Torte."

"Or a Punch Cake to smash."

After Hershko left, Isaak took an Esterházy Cream Torte from one of the side shelves his father had built during his breakdown. He put the pastry on the counter and thumped it. "Shoshana's right. It does feel great to smash a good man." He moved to the front of the shop and removed his shirt. He grabbed the Dobos Torte he had nearly chosen on the first day. He ran the cake across his chest. He stayed near the window. "I don't care if anybody sees."

Isaak imagined he was dancing at the Medzhybizh Town Hall. His head went back and he laughed. He ran his hands over his body. He did a few laps of the shop, swinging his hips and waving his arms in the air. When he again reached the front of the store, he looked through the gap in the window where the Punch Cake had been. "I can do this," he said to himself.

11 🎂 Nina Brodsky Explains Why She was so Satisfied

The gold trimmings on the orbs that crowned the two towers of the Great Synagogue seemed brighter that evening. Isaak thought, "A slice of shame has been lifted from the world and everything is a little lighter. Imagine how things would sparkle if we could rid ourselves of that terrible emotion."

Shoshana was sitting on the couch, waiting for Isaak to complete his nightly commune with the towers. A few strands of hair were out of place and there were dark rings under her eyes. "I tossed and turned last night," she said. "I was frightened I would never have my buttercream moment."

"Shoshana, the story of the Dobos Torte makes it sound so easy. The apprentice makes a mistake, József seizes the opportunity, and everyone lives happily ever after. There are dark parts of ourselves that we must face. The only people who seem to have gotten away with it are József and mother. Stop her if she starts baking a Dobos Torte. That would be gloating. Tell her to cook a Marzipan Cake instead."

"Isaak, you're now a cake man in all senses of the word. But I live in a pastry wasteland. I may never find my cake."

"I never thought I'd say this," said Isaak, "but pastries may not be the answer for everyone. Aliza Lövy called our shop a cake cave. That worked for me, but you might have to go into the world. You're so radiant because you're a woman of the sun. Imagine that. Becoming a better person without a cake in sight."

"That's not going to happen in a hurry. Here's mother with a Fifteen Layer Russian Honey Cake."

As she placed the cake on the table, Nina said, "I couldn't sleep last night. I had to get up and bake."

"Having to make a Fifteen Layer Russian Honey Cake before you can nod off," said Isaak. "That's a big ask for anyone."

"First having to blend all that honey and flour in a bowl," said Shoshana.

"Dividing it into fifteen portions and rolling them into disks," said Isaak.

"Baking them until they're hard," said Shoshana.

"Oh, you two," said Nina.

"Come on, mother," said Isaak.

"Placing the first disk on a plate and covering it with ample quantities of sour cream frosting," said Nina. "Putting the next disk on the first and covering it with more frosting. And so on, until all fifteen are stacked on top of each other. Then leaving it overnight so the frosting seeps into the disks, flavouring and softening them." She smiled. "It's good to play along with you two."

"The Kugelhopf said you had a second chance to be my big breasted mother," said Isaak. "What does the Fifteen Layer Russian Honey Cake say?"

"I can't tell you how much I love this cake world you've introduced us to," said Nina. "It's liberating to think of yourself as pastry and cream, rather than flesh and blood. You start as a big Kugelhopf breast and who knows where you'll end up." She patted Isaak on the leg, communicating her appreciation. "I went back to bed and felt the frosted icing soaking through me, loosening me up inside. I then had the most amazing insight. There's a rigidity to constantly living in bliss. Every day you're stubbornly the same. You think you've worked life out, but that's a trap.

"Suddenly, all sorts of dissatisfactions rose in me. I felt angry. Then, a little sad. I even wondered if I'd wasted my life in ecstasy. It was a relief to be agitated. I woke up ready to take the next step."

"It's not fair, mother," said Shoshana. "Things always arrive when you need them. The dancing at the Medzhybizh Town Hall. The frosted icing last night. Even being agitated this morning. Isaak told me to go into the world and find myself. I'm thankful for his advice. But the world always lands in your lap."

"I'm sorry. And this evening's story is going to irritate you even more."

Nina cut three slices of Fifteen Layer Russian Honey Cake. They each took a bite and returned the slices to their plates.

"I got a job cleaning in the Castle District," said Nina. "It was a long walk from Angyalföld, but I loved it. The beauty of Margit Island made me homesick for Medzhybizh. I missed my old relationship with Yaakov. We started to grow apart on our wedding day and never found our way back to each other. I would cry as I walked past those trees. They were good tears. As if I was watering a forest inside me.

"I'd then reach Parliament House. The fort at Medzhybizh is big and square, with huge walls that no army could penetrate. The soldiers rode out to attack the Ottomans, then took refuge in the castle. Parliament House is all arches and spires reaching to the sky, as if you don't have to worry about the Turks creeping up on you. It touched me that I was in a country where the major building was constructed for beauty, rather than security.

Nina looked at her daughter. "You know, Shoshana, for Isaak, it's cake. For me, it was Margit Island and Parliament House."

"Opera and paintings for Mr Kubrinszky," said Isaak. "For Mrs Davidovitis, Café Noé and the Flódni. The Kazinczy Synagogue for Aliza Lövy. The building, not the congregation."

"It's out there Shoshana," Nina said. "You just have to find it."

It is not easy to be considered unlucky when you are as beautiful as Shoshana. Still, she appreciated her mother and brother's efforts. She picked up her slice of Fifteen Layer Russian Honey Cake and looked at the tiers, softened by the cream frosting. She said, "There's always more than meets the eye."

"Maybe you need fifteen eyes to see the whole person," Isaak said.

"Two should be plenty," said Shoshana. "As long as you are prepared to see more than what you're looking for. Come on, mother. On with this terrible story."

"It was a year after your father and I reached Budapest. We were still living in Angyalföld and had not had sex. Your father was too defeated to get an erection. I didn't mind. The energy unleashed at the Medzhybizh Town Hall was stirring inside me. I liked the tension. It pulsed in my lower abdomen. Then it would suddenly wash through me.

"I glowed, and the city was smitten. People scrutinised my face. I was pretty, but that was not the source of my beauty. They let their eyes wander over my body. Unable to discover why they were entranced, they glared at me, as if I was hiding something. Which, of course, I was.

"I again put my need for sensual pleasure before your father. I couldn't work all day, then sit in a hovel with a depressed man. I went to the Király Baths, down the hill from where I was cleaning. They were built by the Turks during their occupation of the city. A multi domed roof sat above an octagonal ceiling. Small hexagonal openings allowed beams of light to play on the surface of the eight-sided pool. They were old and no one went there. I was so filled by people staring at me, I needed a place to find myself. I understand Shoshana. I really do.

"I adored how the warm waters wrapped around me. It was like being back at the Medzhybizh Town Hall, in a gentler way. At first, I wore a swimming costume. Soon I swam naked, holding my bathers in my hand. I'd never done anything like that before, but the water was like a thousand fingers brushing my skin. I started placing my costume next to the pool. I soon left it in a niche with my clothes. The day came when I forgot it altogether.

"The pool was lit only by a small number of candles. I don't know if management was saving money, or wanted to create an intimate ambience. Whatever the reason, I did not see Miss Sipos until she was at the water's edge. She was so slight her breasts scarcely interrupted the fall of her chest. Her hips caused only a slight detour along the sharp edge of her body. Her bottom was like two small fists. She hardly disturbed the pool as she moved toward me.

"Miss Sipos was the only child of a rich family that lived near the Buda Castle. It was expected she'd marry a man who'd improve the family's status. 'A prince would be just the ticket,' her father said, only partially in jest. The men Miss Sipos was to give her life to had been raised to achieve many goals. None included loving their wives. 'I'll die before I marry a man who wants a sow to spawn his piglets,' she said.

"I told her about my sexless marriage and the pulsing in my pubic area. I whispered that I'd been tempted to relieve the pressure by touching myself, but that would interfere with what was happening inside me. 'I'm afraid I might lose something,' I said.

"'You know your body spiritually,' Miss Sipos said. 'That's very rare.' She explained that living without sex meant solving the problem of how to be an erotically charged woman without going mad. She'd read many learned texts, mainly from Asia. 'Europeans don't like to talk about sex, particularly women's sex,' she said. 'However, I think I've discovered the answer to our dilemma.'

"She explained that we had to stand so close together we'd be in physical contact. I would then take a deep breath. Rather than just breathing absentmindedly, as we usually do, I had to concentrate on the air passing through my throat and filling my chest. My belly would inflate, then I was to imagine the breath going down to my genitals.

"Of course, I found this shocking. However, I understood that Miss Sipos was exploring something important. We were in this together, like the dancers at Medzyhbizh Town Hall. She told me the breath was then to be transferred to her vagina." Nina shook her head. "I know this is a lot to take in.

"The breath would then travel up Miss Sipos's body, swelling her belly and expanding her chest, before moving up through her throat. Instead of exiting her mouth, it would rise to the centre of her forehead, where it would pass back to me. Our bodies would be joined in a circle of breath. From her studies, Miss Sipos was confident our sexual drives would be transformed into a spiritual energy. And I'd believed the whole world was your father looking lovingly at me.

"I was worried someone might come. Miss Sipos said the sacredness of our venture protected us. 'It creates a boundary, shielding us from the outside world.' I must have looked unconvinced. 'Or it might be that families are home having dinner,' she said, 'while younger people are dealing with their sexual needs elsewhere.' We both laughed.

"Miss Sipos drew me to her so our foreheads met. She thrust her pelvis forward, and grabbed my bottom and tilted my hips so our pubes touched. My body stiffened. I shook my head, and said, 'I can't do this.'

"'Just breathe,' said Miss Sipos.

"'I'm the woman that danced at the Medzhybizh Town Hall,' I said.

"'You are.'

"I started well. I felt the breath glide down my throat. However, when my chest expanded, our nipples touched and I gasped, releasing all my air. I was afraid Miss Sipos would be disappointed. She said, 'You did well.'

"All the ache that had accumulated since the Medzhybizh Town

Hall suddenly broke free. I placed my head on her shoulder and cried uncontrollably. Completely spent, I lifted my head and apologised. She said, 'We could be sacrificing our lives making men happy.'

"'You're so kind,' I said. We climbed out of the pool, dressed and went home.

"The next day, I was impatient to get back to the bathhouse. I arrived early, but was still disappointed that Miss Sipos was not there. I was worried my crying had upset her. I could not stand still, so I entered the water.

"I planted my feet on the tiles and began to breathe. The air felt warm in my throat. It then filled my chest. It was when my belly became generously plump that I missed my companion. I longed for the touch of her stomach. I kept going and my breath spread through the folds and cavities of my genitals, softly caressing previously untouched places. I nearly gasped, but maintained my discipline, breathing into my absent partner.

"The air went up through my friend's body until it reached the middle of her forehead. It then came back to me. My pubic region suddenly was hot and pulsating. The reservoir broke. The heat rushed through me and exploded out the top of my head. I felt I was floating away. From a distance, I heard a deep moan. I realised it was me. I fell forward. Miss Sipos caught me. I have no idea how long she'd been there.

"Our breathing climaxes became increasingly explosive. We would leave our bodies and drift off into a realm that was filled with beautiful colours. I could sit happily in the flat all those years because I'd spent so much time in paradise."

Isaak said, "I thought it was dancing at the Medzhybizh Town Hall."

"I imagined it was the Syrniki your mother served you and father," said Shoshana. "Even though it was only in your head."

"When we came back to earth," Nina continued, "Miss Sipos and I would not speak. It was like no words would do justice to our experience. We'd quietly gather the clothes we'd scattered in our rush to find each other.

"In time, we started experimenting. Rather than creating a circle of breath, we breathed forehead to forehead, genital to genital, belly button to belly button, big toe to big toe, noting how each body part created a different sensation, spiritually and emotionally. Then came the night of the heart. We both knew this would be the ultimate climax, if you know what

I mean. We stood in front of each other and breathed through gentle sobs. There were no spectacular colours. Just a soft warmth. We hugged, and my friend kissed me on the forehead. We silently left.

"The next evening, fully dressed, we watched dozens of people bathing in our pool. I told Miss Sipos I was ready to have a baby. She said, 'I'm rich. I'll set you and Yaakov up so you don't have to worry about money. She bought these premises and hired a cook to teach Yaakov to bake. The night we left Angyalföld, Yaakov and I lost our virginity.

"The breathing process had strengthened my vaginal muscles. Even a man in complete control of his climax would have been no match for my python grip. My body pumped every drop of semen onto my eggs. I was pregnant before Yaakov withdrew.

"That was obviously you, Shoshana. I've always thought you were so beautiful because you were conceived in a womb made special by my breathing with Miss Sipos.

"Even when you were a baby, people wanted to kiss you. I fought to give you space, but they got angry with me."

"They wanted me from the start?"

"Yes, love. You've been fighting this battle for a long time."

"Thank you. That helps."

"Then you came along Isaak. Shoshana had taken everything and my womb had gone back to normal. People rushed past you as they flung themselves at your sister. I decided I could not fill you with love, just for the whole world to snub you. It was safer if you were rejected by me. I never returned your smiles. I showed no excitement when you crawled or walked. I denied you every step of the way. I made you into a Chimney Cake. Empty in the middle so you wouldn't feel the world's dismissal. I still think it was for the best. And now you're filling out in the most exciting way."

Isaak was stunned. As was now his habit in these situations, he said the first thing that came into his head. "Mother, I'm afraid I might be an Apple Strudel. Soft in the middle and flaky on the outside?"

"No, silly! You'll be a Fifteen Layer Russian Honey Cake. All those different levels of you, making you a whole person."

"I hope I don't get eaten alive."

"Watch out," Shoshana said. "Not all the girls are perfect Krémes. Some are Punch Cakes looking for a bit of fun. 'Here's a Fifteen Layer Russian Honey Cake. Wouldn't mind getting my teeth into that.'"

"I better make sure a few of my disks stay hard."

"The top and bottom. You could be a bit mushy in the middle."

"A Fifteen Layer Russian Honey Cake with Apple Strudel filling."

"The perfect man!"

They both laughed.

Nina said, "I love watching you two. Maybe it's time for me to eat a Punch Cake and loosen up a little."

"As long as there's no dancing," said Isaak.

"No naked breathing," said Shoshana.

"I know, I'm not going to bake any more cakes. I'll buy wonderful pastries, the best I can find. That would be fun. It feels so free."

"And safe," said Isaak.

Nina put her hand up to stop the talking. "How did I miss it," she said. "That time with Miss Sipos opened something up in me. I not only went off into the universe and saw those amazing colours, I could also tune into things here, on earth. That's how I knew all about the cakes, Isaak. It was almost as if I was in your head."

"I'm not sure I like that."

"But that's what the pastries are doing for you. Taking you into people's minds. Where would you be without that? Where would any of us be?"

"We all need to breathe," said Shoshana. "And someone to breathe with."

Isaak relented. "As long as it's in the privacy of our home."

12 ♟ Hershko Kubrinszky Returns for a Last Cake-analytic Session

The next morning, Isaak looked around the cakes, still stacked on the shelves. He thought, "I'm sorry, father. You lost your way when mother started dancing. I hope you make it back." The door opened and Hershko Kubrinszky walked in. "I was having a quiet time with my father," Isaak complained. "Even if it was only in my head."

"It's good you're talking to your father," said Hershko. "But we have work to do. I came for a cake that you don't stock and never will. It's a cut above anything you sell."

"You've mixed us up with the mad turkeys at the Auguszt Café. Isn't that where you were planning to go?"

"I've been giving some thought to this pastry stuff," said Hershko. "What if it has nothing to do with actually purchasing a cake? In the future, people might go to an empty shop and simply ask for the cake they would have bought. The time might come when they don't mention cakes at all. They'll just discuss their problems."

"How would the cake seller make money?"

"They'd be paid to listen and offer wise counsel. I don't mean to offend you, but your pastries are pretty average. This is the only shop in the quarter where no one buys a cake. Has anyone actually eaten one since you've been here?"

"I've tried a few and they're pretty good," Isaak lied. "Anyway, what you're saying doesn't make sense. You needed to actually smash the Punch. It would not have been enough to squash it in your mind. Or simply tell me that's what you wanted to do. You needed a real cake and a real fist. Otherwise, it's all just in your head."

"But what if it is in your head? What if I didn't have to wet myself at the Iron Gates? What if I could just tell someone I was scared."

"That's the problem. There was no possibility of you telling anyone. You couldn't even admit it to yourself. It was the piddle that said you were frightened."

"That's true. But it still might be possible to avoid all that. Maybe your ultimate purpose is to help us save on laundry bills." He laughed. "It's got to come out but does it have to be so physical? Do you really want to spend your life cleaning up after customers."

"What if it's the seller that needs the cakes? What if the pastries help him to get it right? You wanted a Dobos. The cakes told me you needed the Punch."

"The cake man would talk to other patisserie owners. He'd tell them about his customers and describe what he was doing to assist them. They'd help him think about what was happening, and make sure he didn't lose his way. They'd work together. You wouldn't be so reliant on the cakes."

It always amazed me that people who had suffered highly traumatic childhoods, folk you would expect to angrily turn against the world, often managed to keep a core of goodness in their hearts. It was as if they had sealed that aspect of themselves behind thick walls, keeping it secure until it could be safely introduced into a more caring environment. I would say there had always been a part of Hershko beyond his rage. That was why he was touched by the ship owner talking about his father, and the opera and Jacob Bogdany's paintings. At some level, he always knew he could be a better person. Hershko did not need to win the argument that day, even though he knew he was right. Isaak had given him so much. He could let him be. He said, "Today's cake is a Walnut Crepe with Chocolate Sauce, as served at Gundel's."

Gundel Restaurant was on the western edge of City Park, close to the centre of downtown Pest. Most patrons accessed it by walking along Andrássy utca, a tree-lined boulevard built in 1872 as a celebration of the city's coming of age. The street is lined with stately neo-Renaissance mansions and boasts the State Opera House and the Hungarian University of Fine Arts. It is a Budapest tradition to stroll along Andrássy, letting your heart swell with nationalistic pride. "Austrians walk aimlessly around the Ringstrasse," goes a famous Hungarian saying. "We walk straight up Andrássy."Given its position, Károly Gundel had no option but to create a spectacular establishment. Gundel's ceilings were high, the walls wood panelled, and the floors artfully tiled. The restaurant was decorated with pleasant paintings, such as Dezső Orbán's, "Still Life with Pear" and Aladár Kőrösfői-Kriesch's, "Outdoor Gathering".

A quality restaurant needs a signature dish and it was here that Károly Gundel revealed his eccentric genius. Rather than compete with the city's great chefs, he embraced his limitations. He risked everything on the simple crepe, a taken-for-granted treat that a child could cook. He transformed it into Gundel's Walnut Crepe with Chocolate Sauce. Budapest connoisseurs enthused, "It combines the playfulness of childhood with adult sophistication. It both challenges the fundamentals of Budapest baking, while moving the Hungarian pastry project forward. It encourages light-heartedness, while inspiring serious reflection on where we are as a nation."

"The thing is, I don't actually need a Walnut Crepe with Chocolate Sauce," Hershko Kubrinszky said. "I already know what the cake means for me. But I've come to realise it's not enough to understand who we are. We're communal beings. We need to reveal ourselves to others. It's the only path to true happiness."

It is always difficult for a therapist when the patient moves beyond him. Hershko now had a wider vision of Cake-analysis, and of life, than Isaak. It was only to be expected that Isaak felt exposed.

At these times, the therapist must remain humble, and stay true to the process. He has to acknowledge the steps the patient is taking, while staying in touch with the client's inner world. Unfortunately, Isaak had not yet developed this capacity. He said, "Mr Kubrinszky. You come to my shop and ask for a cake I don't have, already knowing what it means for you. I have better things to do than play silly games."

Hershko burst out laughing. "I don't need a Punch Cake to have fun. Listening to you make stupid statements is more than enough. Better things to do. If I wasn't here, you'd be going mad."

"I'd be getting on with my life."

"You're stuck here. At least for the time being."

"How do you know this?"

"People think angry men just blast away, wiping everybody out. They're wrong. You've got to read people. I knew you'd come out swinging."

"That's why I didn't land a punch."

"Yes. And now I'm realising I can look past the fighter and into every part of the person. It's a wonderful gift. You've helped me claim it, just by being you."

"But you're moving on," said Isaak. "The same will happen with Mrs Davidovitis and Aliza Lövy. Meanwhile, I'm stuck here. What if no one else comes? What if new people come? I'd just have to go through it all again. I lose either way."

"I understand. But you have to see it through. Leave now and you'll just go round swinging punches. This is your training ring. Get yourself fighting fit for the battles ahead."

"Tell me this. I'm the one doing the cake stuff, but everyone seems to know me better than I do. How does that work?"

"I think the cakes chose you because you were the most naïve person in the quarter. There wasn't enough of you to get in the road when they needed someone to speak through. Who else would have been mad enough to tell me to have more fun?"

"That's what they'll put on my gravestone," said Isaak. 'There wasn't enough of him to get in the road.'"

"Don't be such a sook. This cake thing has been good for me, and for others. But you'll be the one who gets the most out of it. Your headstone will say, "The cakes got him started."

"You better tell me about Gundel's Walnut Crepe with Chocolate Sauce. Then get out of my shop so I can get on with my training. I don't want to be here forever."

"Here's my story. Even though I don't have a cake."

"Get on with it."

"I first visited Gundel's after the successful run to Bucharest. My fees were exorbitant but I'd shown I was up for the job. Rich clients shook my hand, called me sir and told me I was a good man. It didn't affect me. My lunch was still a roughly cut meat sandwich, scoffed down in my dirty shipping office.

"Then I'm at a business lunch at Gundel's, eating Duck Trio—duck three ways—with braised cabbage and apple, a truffle-enriched celery puree, and egg brioche toast. This might sound odd, but I didn't know the difference between a Duck Trio and a greasy meat sandwich. Food was just something you stuffed in your mouth.

"Suddenly, there was a voice in my head saying, 'Take your time, Hershko. Let yourself enjoy it. You deserve this.' I chewed slowly and started to notice the subtle flavours of the duck three ways. This was a greater victory than roaring through the Iron Gates. That was just my anger doing what it always did. I was now becoming rich on the inside. The waiter brought a Walnut Crepe with Chocolate Sauce and I wanted to throw it at him.

"The message, 'Success comes through hard work,' had been carved into my soul. But Károly Gundel had turned an everyday cake into a classic. The rich know how easy it can be." He started to cry. "It didn't have to be so hard. I could have taken it easy and let it all work out."

There were times in my practice when I could not stay in the reflective space. Something snapped, and I would angrily tell the patient who they were and how they kept wrecking their lives. There is no doubt this stemmed from my limitations as a therapist, and as a person. Later, I would think, "What have I done?" However, the client usually appreciated these moments. They could see my compassion was genuine. They realised someone could be angry with them but still care. It is part of being a therapist. You often do your best work when you fail.

Isaak had one of those moments. "So, Mr Kubrinszky. You didn't have to wet yourself in the middle of the Iron Gates. You didn't have to smash a Punch Cake. You didn't even have to be an angry man. You could waltz out of Angyalföld and into Gundel's without missing a beat. The rich know it's easy because it is easy, for them. József Dobos could discover buttercream because he wasn't a struggling patisserie owner who couldn't afford mistakes. Don't kid yourself it could have been painless. I'll tell you one thing. I'll never sell a Walnut Crepe with Chocolate Sauce in this shop. Nothing here will ever be easy."

"You're right. I shouldn't sell myself short."

"Don't do that!"

"This time, I won't be coming back."

"Get out of here. But first tell me if I'm through the Iron Gates?"

Hershko sighed. "I'm sorry. It's getting closer. Just be patient."

That evening, Isaak stood outside the pantry door. He said, "Father, running a cake shop is hard work. Thank you for keeping it going all those years." He thought he heard his father weeping.

13 ♔ Shoshana Brodsky Ventures into the World

Isaak only looked briefly at the two towers that evening. It was now more a habit than a need for connection. He looked round to find his sister in her usual place on the three-seater couch. She looked tired, but happy.

Shoshana said, "I went for a long walk today. I caught people's eye. I even smiled. Of course, they melted. That's fine. What's important is no one thrust into me. It was like moving through a sexless city."

"That's wonderful. One day you might push into them."

"I've been thinking about that. The thing is, I have no idea what I'd do once I was in there."

It is useful to think of psychotherapy as a series of vacuums. It is in these voids that the patient finds what they need, and the therapist discovers what they can offer. The same applies to life. Shoshana's confusion provided the space for Isaak to realise something important. He said, "For love, Shoshana. For someone to help you grow. Mr Kubrinszky has been inside me, and me in him. In a good way. He came to the shop for the last time today. We've given each other all we've got. At least for the time being. I can already feel him slipping out of me. But we will always be part of each other. That's why you get inside someone, and let someone inside of you. It's risky, but life's empty if you don't try."

"That's beautiful, but I'd like more time with nobody in me, and me in no one else. For better or worse."

"I understand. I wish I had taken longer. Got to know myself better while it was just me. But it's alright."

"I went for a long walk today and ended up at the Anonymous Statue in City Park," said Shoshana. "It's supposed to be Master P., the chronicler of the Court of Bela III. His face is covered by his cloak as he sits writing his notes. It's like he's part of everything around him, but also removed. That's what I want to be, for now."

Isaak smiled. "I understand."

"After spending time with the Anonymous Statue, I walked through the city to Vörösmarty tér. I don't know if you've ever really looked at the statue in the centre of the park. The great Vörösmarty sits high on a plinth. He's slightly bent forward as he reflects on the human condition. I could sense his empathy, and why he wrote such wonderful plays and poetry.

"Below Vörösmarty are a number of different family groups, set out around the column. Life's tough, but their affection for one another is obvious. I thought how close you and I have become. And mother, too. I hope father comes out of the cupboard and joins us. I might even have my own family one day. I'd prefer that to being Mihály Vörösmarty, sitting above the world.

"Oh, by the way. While I was in the park, I saw mother go into Gerbeauds. She bowled straight in as if she owned the place."

Café Gerbeaud, established in 1870, was designed to rival the best coffee houses in Paris and Vienna. It features a high ceiling, adorned with chandeliers. The walls are wood panelled and the tables are topped with marble. A long front window opens onto Vörösmarty tér.

Nina entered and placed three beautiful cakes on the coffee table. "I told you I wouldn't be baking anymore," she said. "I went to Café Noé, following in Mrs Davidovitis's footsteps. The place was too small and the Flódnis looked about to fall over. Then I went to the Auguszt Café. It was in uproar. A customer would call out a word and others responded with whatever came into their heads. "I yelled Syrniki. The first comments were dismissive. 'Old days,' 'shtetl,' 'Russians,' 'pogroms.' Then it turned. 'Summer.' 'Making do.' 'Mother.' Everyone went quiet. I said, 'Even mad turkeys need their mothers. Particularly their mad turkey mothers.' They cheered.

"I left feeling confident I could hold my own with you two, though you'll probably still be too quick for me."

"I thought you did pretty good," said Isaak.

"Like a bird on the wing."

"The flightless turkey takes off."

"See what I mean," said Nina. "Anyway, I marched out of the Auguszt Café buzzing with energy. I stormed across the Chain Bridge to the Király's Baths. I nearly went inside, but it would be very different without Miss Sipos. I crossed the river at the Margit Bridge. I called out, 'The Turks might have destroyed your church, little Margit, but your trees are beautiful.' I then walked to Parliament House. I actually felt Christian. I would have sung a hymn, but I don't know any. I made do with an old Yiddish folksong.

"As I walked, I realised my breathing with Miss Sipos was just another period of my life. It didn't have to define who I was. The realisation made me feel stronger. I walked into Gerbeauds like I belonged. I sat by the window and drank a cup of coffee. I saw you sitting in the park, Shoshana. I waved, but you didn't see me. You seemed lost in your thoughts.

"As I sat in the cafe, I realised my Syrniki and Kugelhopf days were over."

"You might never bake another Syrniki, mother," said Isaak, "but it feels like we're sitting on the porch at Medzhybizh."

"That's true. The other thing that happened today was I realised how much I wanted to share my life with your father. I've got to get him out of the pantry and onto the dance floor."

"What about just into your arms," said Isaak.

"Yes, mother," said Shoshana, "that's an image we don't need."

14 🎂 Keila Davidovitis Returns to Brodsky's

Two fantasies competed for Isaak's mind as he walked down the stairs to the shop the next morning. In the first, word of Hershko Kubrinszky's transformation had spread through the quarter. "The angry man has been tamed," people were saying. "His greetings are now long and relaxed, as if he could spend the whole day smiling. Whatever happened in Brodsky's, I want some myself." A large crowd would be waiting eagerly outside the shop. In the other daydream, the mob were furious. They shouted, "If he can turn Hershko Kubrinszky into a smiling idiot, what could he do to us!"

Of course, no one was outside the store. Of all the things that create mass excitement, deep psychological change is way down the list. In fact, the more Hershko offered his generous smile, the greater was the unconscious backlash against Brodsky's. A genuinely happy person threatened to reveal the shallowness of the quarter's positivity, and expose the underlying pain. Even when the unconscious wins, it loses.

Isaak was glad there were no customers waiting for him. He took it as a sign he could leave the shop. He would spend the morning clearing the cakes from the shelves, and that would be it.

Isaak Brodsky never did wet himself in the patisserie. However, as he worked his way through that final task, he broke down and sobbed. "The cakes have given me so much. I feel like I'm throwing part of myself away." By the time he had finished, he felt lighter, as if his tears had flushed Cake-analysis out of his system. He was ready for a new life.

There is another reason why people are disinclined to give over to the unconscious. Once you have allowed the psyche to take control, you cannot reclaim your life until it decides you are ready. Isaak marched triumphantly to the door and grabbed the handle. He could not turn it. He looked at his hand in frustration, but he knew the problem was his head. "Damn!" he yelled. "My sister and Mr Kubrinszky were right." He stormed back to the middle of the store.

Now that Hershko Kubrinszky had ended his Cake-analysis, it now fell to Keila Davidovitis to intervene. She came into the shop pulling a covered trolley behind her. She sensed that Isaak was upset but ignored his irritation. She said, "It's wonderfully quiet in here. I didn't realise the cakes were so noisy."

"They never shut up."

"Without saying a word."

"Without opening their non-existent mouths."

"It's going to be hard bringing them back."

"I can tell you one thing, Mrs Davidovitis. The pastries are not coming back. In fact, Mr Kubrinszky believes we don't need them anymore. Don't forget that you went all the way to urination without actually purchasing a cake."

"I have the greatest respect for Mr Kubrinszky. Just yesterday, he grinned with a generosity I've never witnessed before. You helped him escape the Roulade."

"He never chose that cake."

"He should have. He was as stuck as anybody. It was you that solved the riddle of that terrible pastry." She nodded her appreciation.

"There could be some truth in what Mr Kubrinszky is saying," Keila continued. "One day, psychological work might be done without a pastry in sight. But we both know that's not the reason you don't want the cakes back. I know you want out of here. But take it from me, it's easy to get ahead of yourself and end up trapped in a Chocolate Chestnut Roulade of your own making. Next time, you might not get out."

"Those loud-mouthed pastries were out of control," said Isaak. "What happened with you and Mr Kubrinszky seemed fun at the time. But looking back, it was all very distressing. And Aliza Lövy gets goosebumps and I never see her again." He lowered his voice. "Just between you and me, I feel used."

"I know. You thought you'd give a girl goosebumps and she'd be yours. It doesn't work that way."

"I wouldn't mind being a Cake-analyst with old people, like you and Mr Kubrinszky."

"Thank you."

"But it would cause problems with people my age. Aliza didn't really see me as a man. I was just someone to get her to where she needed to go. To be frank, so did you and Mr Kubrinszky. Did he notice it was my cake he was smashing? Did you stop to think who's floor you were pissing on? I got a taste for how Shoshana feels."

"I know you're upset, but peeing on your floor has helped me see things. I looked at my Flódni at Café Noé the other day, and thought, 'It's not about pulling the layers apart. The Flódni tells us everything is connected. Every tier is in tune with the others.' I then realised the Flódni is a symbol for the world. It's all linked. My mind was moving smoothly from one idea to the next. Berko's efforts at the Auguszt Café were not in vain."

"My mother was there yesterday. She said the association game is very popular. She called out Syrniki. The first responses were disappointing, but it worked out in the end."

"That's wonderful. One day I'll go back to the Auguszt in honour of my brave husband. But right now, I have to tell you my amazing insight." Keila paused for dramatic effect. "There was a relationship between the madness of your father's display and the crazy things that happened in this shop. The window spoke to us. It said we had to explore our own insanity. We walked in ready to go mad. That's when I realised all displays talk to the mind of the customer. Everybody thinks they're just contemplating the pastries. They're actually in deep conversation with the window.

"I left Noé's and walked around the quarter, stopping to consider how the windows spoke to their patrons. You know what they say? 'I'm not interested in you beyond selling a cake.' Sadly, most customers reply, 'That's fine. I'll take a pastry and be on my way.'

"There were times when it all went seriously wrong. I saw desperate people walking back and forward in front of windows. Do they need a big chocolate cake to blast an intense feeling of sadness? Or something subtle and nurturing? They are the real casualties of the cake industry's indifference. Of course, it's no use expecting cake men to change. They're stubborn people who believe the nation owes them."

"Do you think they'll be blamed if Hungary loses the war?"

"The day is coming when mothers tell their sons to be lawyers and doctors, not chefs."

"As desperate as that."

"I've been reflecting on how a great display would speak to the customer." She pulled the cover away from the trolley. "I've brought the cakes you need for your window."

Isaak sighed.

"I know you've had enough, but this will be your last step in getting out of here."

"Will it get me through the Iron Gates?"

"I don't know. But it will get you somewhere."

Isaak shook his head. "I'm starting to understand that's as good as it gets."

15 🎂 Keila Davidovitis Creates the Cake-analytic Display Window

Keila said, "There's a fundamental enigma at the heart of the window that every patisserie owner must address—a great cake display starts with the humble biscuit. No one buys them spontaneously. Men never purchase biscuits. Housewives stay loyal to a small number of favourites, or are happy to accord with their guests' preferences. Yet, paradoxically, the biscuit is the foundation on which the window is built. Because you are not trying to turn customers into rabid biscuit purchasers, or attempting to convince them that a biscuit will meet their emotional needs, they must be placed inconspicuously on the top shelf. Do that, and your customers will feel understood. They'll fall in love with you immediately, especially the women." Mrs Davidovitis looked softly into the distance, imagining a world filled with thoughtful bakers, all in touch with the inner needs of their female clientele.

"It would be completely inappropriate to watch your sister wake each morning. Just imagine a lioness, stretching like a big cat in the grasslands. She wiggles her toes and rolls her shoulders. She straightens her arms behind her head. The morning stretch is the transition from withdrawing into ourselves to venturing into the universe. The majority of your customers are female. Put the top shelf a little above the eye line of the average woman. It will encourage an agreeable extension. She'll then be pleasantly aroused as she contemplates the rest of the display.

"My body has been clamped tight since Berko died. Now, I'm starting to unwind." She lifted herself onto the balls of her feet and raised her hands over her head. She encouraged Isaak to do the same.

"Despite everything I've said about biscuit buying predictability," Keila continued after they had completed their stretch, "you must challenge your customer. You might have a lioness in front of your window, but a frightened kitten in the shop.

"Scared of embarrassing themselves in front of their friends, or believing they should live unchanging lives, including eating the same biscuit at precisely ten each morning, housewives stick rigidly to the tried and true. It's a paralysis I know too well. A dead-end place where the purchasing experience is diminished to buying the same old biscuits from a shop that is chosen for its convenient location. What should be a thrilling engagement with the world becomes a living death. The Chocolate Chestnut Roulade is everywhere." Keila suddenly looked sad. "Who am I to talk?" she said. "I spent my life trapped in the Roulade. Then suddenly I'm at the Auguszt Café, acting like I'm a Dobos Torte. The thing is, I wasn't trying to break free. In fact, I didn't even know I was stuck. Berko looked so lost and alone, I just had to rescue him. But I couldn't stop myself talking."

It would have been easy for Isaak to take advantage of Keila's vulnerability. He could have said, "Mrs Davidovitis, this window is obviously bringing up painful feelings. I shudder to think what it will do to the people of the quarter. Let's leave things as they are. I'll close the shop."

As a baby, Isaak would have been devastated by his mother's refusal to connect with him. However, I suspect at some level in his psyche, he sensed his mother's lack of response was an act of care. Despite everything, he knew he was a loved human being. That was why he could take advantage of what Cake-analysis offered him, and allow himself to be a better man. He said, "Mrs Davidovitis, it's terrible that Berko couldn't bear you bursting into life at the Auguszt Café. But we know you were acting from kindness. You couldn't stay stuck in the Chocolate Chestnut Roulade. That would have killed you, and Berko. You had no choice. And look where you are now, creating this wonderful window. Your mad turkey's not to blame. It's come home to roost."

Keila saw herself through Isaak's eyes—a good woman, intelligent and strong. She said, "We're going to start with the Kipfel. It's very ordinary, but that's the point."

Is there anything more powerful than watching someone go down into their pain, then make their way back out, while knowing you have been crucial to their recovery? Isaak felt emotionally open. He said, "You know, in a way, I've had it much easier than Shoshana."

"You have. You're lucky you're not beautiful."

"I'll take that as a compliment."

Keila said, "You might not know this, but in 1683, the Turks became frustrated in their two month siege of Vienna and started tunnelling under the city wall. However, the chefs, working in their underground bakeries heard the burrowing and raised the alarm. The Viennese were able to stall the Ottomans till the arrival of the Poles and Bavarians. The bakers commemorated the victory by creating pastries in the shape of the crescent on the Turkish flag. The French have their sloppy croissant. Our Kipfel is tidy and sophisticated.

"I know the Kipfel isn't really a biscuit. But it's not a cake, either. It's good and solid and associated with keeping Europe free from the marauding Ottoman. The customer will see the Kipfel in the centre of the top shelf and understand she's in safe hands. There will be no madness in this shop."

Keila's comment jolted Isaak. "The days of weeing, punching cakes and goosebumps are over?"

"I'm afraid so. There will be more thinking and less action."

"I might not like that, despite everything I've said."

I would have responded to Isaak with therapeutic empathy. I would have acknowledged that his father's madness, and the insanity in the shop, had ignited his life. It would be frightening to let that go. At the most existential level, could he survive without the stimulation? The hope would be that in recognising his fears, Isaak could move past them.

Keila Davidovitis was more pragmatic. She said, "Isaak, we can put everything back the way it was and you can have all the craziness you want. You might feel more alive, but you'll be digging yourself into a deep hole. The Roulade would win again."

As a rule, these threats tend to disorientate people. They accept the other person is right, but their response feels more impatient than empathic. What Isaak did next is standard for folk in this situation. Unable to put words to his confusion, he nodded weakly, indicating Keila should go on.

"In the early Middle Ages," Keila continued, "Italians baked crisp breads, called Biscotti, by partially cooking the dough as a loaf. They then cut it into slices, which they briefly returned to a cooler oven to crisp. This second baking made the biscuit drier, dramatically extending its life." Keila paused, then said, "Berko used to talk to me like he was reading from an encyclopedia. I'm now doing that to you. It seems he got into my head more than I thought." She shrugged. "Anyway, sugar was introduced to Europe in the sixteenth century, and Tuscans from the city of Prato added it to the Biscotti mix. The biscuit travelled to central Europe, where it was flavoured with bitter almonds and known as Mandelbrot. 'Brot' is both German and Yiddish for bread, and 'mandel' is German and Yiddish for almond.

"Mandelbrot is popular because its longevity means it can be stored for unexpected guests. Mandelbrot is the housewife's friend. We'll place it to the right of the Kipfel.

For most of her adult life, Keila Davidovitis had been limited to two primary facial expressions. One was her look of awe as she listened to Berko. The other communicated her terrible despair after his death. Now she experimented with looking cheeky. She tilted her head to the right, while gazing at Isaak through the top of her right eye. She shaped her mouth into a half smile. "Here's something shocking," she said. "The next biscuit is the Indian Head." Still looking mischievous, she said, "Can you believe it?"

The Hungarian Count, Ferdinand Pálffy, was a prominent engineer in the early nineteenth century. Like many who make their mark in the technical professions, Pálffy was determined to prove he was more than a nuts and bolts man. He tried to demonstrate his aesthetic credentials by purchasing the Theatre der Wien. Unfortunately, Pálffy made the mistake of offering productions that proved his bona fides as a cultured person, rather than those audiences wanted to attend. Grand dramas and operas played to empty stalls.

Pálffy could have stubbornly continued in the same way, while complaining about the city's lack of sophistication. However, his success as an engineer stemmed from his determination to never leave a problem unsolved. He employed an Indian magician, Kotum Bulchia, to provide entertainment before the show and during intervals. The public still stayed away. Pálffy then commanded his chef to create a delicacy that complemented the magician. In the baker's mind, Indians were synonymous with turbans. A ball of jelly roll sponge was sliced in half and filled with whipped cream. The two turban ends were dipped in chocolate. Some people thought the chocolate was too dark for an Indian and referred to the cakes as Moors' Heads.

Depending on which story you believe, people flocked to the theatre to purchase the cakes, stayed for the performance, and all was saved. Or, everyone bought the pastries and went home, leaving the theatre to fail. The irony, given Pálffy's pretensions, is his legacy is a simple pastry that the general public loved and could afford.

"We'll put the Indian Head to the left of the Kipfel," said Keila. She looked at the top shelf and nodded with satisfaction. "We now have three ways the customer can go. The Kipfel is a good solid purchase. The Mandelbrot is also reliable, but the sugar introduces a dash of sweetness, while the almonds add an interesting touch. Then there's the exotic Indian Heads. Imagine serving them at morning tea. Would it bring laughter or scorn?"

The Brodskys were loyal to the Hussar Kisses, a boring thumbprint biscuit with a slight depression at its crown that was filled with a good strawberry jam, or a candied cherry. The biscuits were popular with young women who imagined being seized by a handsome soldier on horseback. Mrs Davidovitis told Isaak she still fantasised about being claimed by a burly man on a horse as big as a truck. "But we're building a new cake world that doesn't play with young girls' minds, or exploit old women's desires," she said. "This morning, the Hussars lose the battle of Rumbach utca."

"Yes," said Isaak making a fist.

Keila made two fists, then leaned back and yelled, "Yes!" She laughed and said, "Oh dear, that was wonderful."

"The window's already working," said Isaak.

"With the top shelf in place," Keila continued, "we now turn to the other two tiers. The fundamentals are the same. What transforms a good display into a great presentation is the tension between conformity and adventure. Your window must include an impressive array of classics, baked in the time-honoured fashion, offering a safe and predictable eating experience. However, it must also challenge your customer, bringing out the best in them. They might be smart, funny, or vivacious. It doesn't matter, as long as the cakes do their job.

"The housewife is touched by the thoughtfulness of the display. She is stimulated by the stretch up to the biscuits. Her gaze drifts downward.

The cake in the middle of the centre shelf must meet her new found expansiveness. This is obviously a buttercream moment. The Dobos Torte must take pride of place in the presentation."

"I understand the greatness of the Dobos," Isaak said. "However, sometimes I think Hungarian baking, and the Hungarian nation, will only come of age when we move past it. The cake carries so much weight, but it also holds us back."

"I understand, Isaak, but for this window to work, it must fit with Hungarian cooking, not change it. It's about transforming people, not baking."

Keila then placed an Esterházy Cream Torte to the right side of the Dobos. "The Dobos tells us to be open to life's fortunate accidents. The Esterházy reminds us to keep trying, even when we've suffered humiliating defeat."

Keila then said, "Here's the next surprise. We'll put the Hazelnut Macaroon Cake to the left of the Dobos."

I again have to interrupt the narrative and say that this was the only time I was confused during my recording of The Interpretation of Cakes. In my experience, a macaroon is a small biscuit made from ground almonds, coconut or other nuts. The Hazelnut Macaroon Cake that Mrs Davidovitis placed in the Brodsky display window was as large as a typical layer cake. It consisted of four crunchy hazelnut flavoured meringue tiers, stacked around a large disk of meringue, with a filling of chocolate cream ganache. How could that be a macaroon?

Fortunately, these nuances did not bother Keila Davidovitis. She said, "The thing about this pastry is the anticipation. The meringues create an edgy feeling in the teeth. It feels dangerous. If someone buys an Indian Head and a slice of Hazelnut Macaroon Cake, you know they're desperate for change."

Isaak nodded. "You seem to be building the presentation like a Flódni, layer by layer."

"That's interesting. My time at Café Noé must have been more productive than I thought."

"Maybe there could be a number of shops," Isaak said, "spread throughout the quarter, each with different windows. The customer could find the display that spoke to them. Or, maybe, we could change this window every day. We would then attract a variety of customers with different psychological issues."

"That's a fascinating idea, but let's stay with the job at hand. The bottom shelf represents one of the world's great ironies. You're dragging your customer away from your premier offerings, to cakes that you consider inferior. You have no choice. The bottom shelf is where customers risk everything and lives are changed. Take that away and all you have is a cake shop.

"There's one sure way to draw the customer's gaze downward," Keila continued. "Everybody wants an Apple Strudel at some point in their life. But that's a conservative option. Put that cake in the centre of the bottom shelf and you're saying Brodsky's ultimately plays it safe. You'll attract people who believe they're looking to change, but ultimately stay the same. It's got to be the Rigó Jancsi Chocolate Mousse Cake. It will transform the quarter forever."

Keila's choice was named for the famous gypsy violinist. It is said that when Jancsi played, his eyes were wild and his hair flew like a horse's mane. His notoriety for fast hands did not just relate to his playing. One evening, he was performing at a prestigious Parisian restaurant when the Baroness Chimay of Belgium stormed the stage. She ripped off her wedding ring, and abandoned her husband and two children to travel the world with the fiddler.

Back in Budapest, Rigó was celebrated as a hero. A gypsy winning a Belgium Baroness confirmed the potency of the Hungarian male. Soon after that fateful night, a Budapest chef strode out of his kitchen and presented his new creation. A sensationally rich chocolate custard and cream mixture was sandwiched between two slices of chocolate-flavoured jelly roll, and topped with chocolate frosting. The chef said, "This cake is so rich, it's scandalous. I have no option but to name it the Rigó Jancsi Chocolate Mousse Cake."

I am sure Keila chose the Rigó Jancsi because she wanted to sexualise the bottom shelf. Customers were to be stimulated, so they would be more willing to take a chance. However, what Keila did not take into account, was the singer did not dump Clara and move on. Nor did Clara say, "Thanks Jancsi, you got me out of that terrible marriage. You go now."

I know what I am saying will create controversy in Budapest. But, in the end, psychotherapy is basically a relationship between two people, brought together under odd circumstances, and doing their best to make it work. As a therapist, you develop an instinct for how couples are formed, and what keeps them together. Keila was wrong. The Rigó Jancsi is not the cake of lust. It is the pastry of love.

16 🎂 The Rigó Jancsi Chocolate Mousse Cake Does the Trick

Aliza had rushed back to the Kazinczy Synagogue after leaving Brodsky's on that first morning. She yelled, "I'm the woman of the goosebumps. I'm the perfect Kréme." What Aliza did not understand was her time with Isaak would kickstart a fundamental realignment of her inner world. Where her life had previously been ruled by her intellect, she would now be emotionally labile. One minute it was great to be alive in a world of endless possibility. Then the slightest provocation would spin her into an explosive fury, or reduce her to a flood of tears.

By the morning after Keila Davidovitis had rearranged the Brodsky window, Aliza was tired of the emotional rollercoaster. She stormed over to the Kazinczy, and yelled, "You should have warned me that goosebumps would turn everything upside down. I want to go back to who I was."

I suspect the Kazinczy's task had been to get Aliza out of her head and into her feelings. As far as it was concerned, its work was finished. For the first time ever, it did not respond.

The Kazinczy's silence created the space for Aliza to make an important discovery. Almost in a whisper, she said, "We have gone as far as we can go. Thank you for everything. I'm heading over to see Isaak. I think he's my perfect Kréme."

Aliza broke out in goosebumps as she stretched to look at the biscuits. She let her eyes wander over the rest of the window, then dashed into the shop. "You've done it," she said. "A wonderful blending of Orthodox and art nouveau. If the Viennese Secessionists ever designed a display, this would be it. Classic Hungarian meets the Kozma utca Cemetery. Give me a slice of Rigó Jancsi."

The Cake-analytic interpretation was straight forward. Isaak thought, "Having discovered goosebumps, you now want to be swept off your feet by someone who can offer you the world." It was the next thought that caused problems. "I want to be that man, but I'm not up to it." Isaak felt himself collapsing. "After all I've been through," he thought, "I still can't sweep a woman off her feet, even when her purchase proves how much she wants me to."

Aliza sensed Isaak was struggling. However, having found the strength to leave the Kazinczy, and to courageously order a cake she could never have bought before, she would not let herself be dragged down by his sadness. "I'm not sure the Secessionist would put the Dobos in the middle of the window," she said. "I think they'd risk the Chocolate Macaroon Cake."

Isaak could feel Aliza reaching inside him, searching for something that matched what was happening in herself. But what could he say? The interpretation was ultimately useless, even though it was correct. He did not dare tell her he wanted to give her the world.

"I like what you've done with the biscuits," Aliza said. "The stretch is very evocative."

It is hard to come face to face with your limitations, to find yourself wandering lost and alone in the vacuum of your inner world, unable to meet the appropriate expectations of others. People often crumble at this moment. They say things like, "I think you're right about the Chocolate Macaroon Cake, Aliza. The Secessionists would love it." They know they are being fraudulent, but it gets them through an awkward moment without exposing their shortcomings. Isaak courageously decided he would stay silent until he had something authentic to say.

Aliza's patience had worn thin. A tremor formed in the lower reaches of her abdomen. It worked its way to her extremities. The paper bag holding the Rigó Jancsi began to rustle furiously. She spat, "The goosebumps man is a one trick pony!" She removed the pastry from the paper bag and placed it on the counter. Isaak thought she was going to smash it.

Aliza said, "Eat this Jancsi slowly and think what it means for a young woman to purchase this cake from a man. If you can't work that out, you'd better put everything back the way it was because you'll never be art nouveau." She stormed out.

Isaak took a bite of the Rigó Jancsi. He immediately spat it out, a great spray that made a mess on the counter. "In his effort to capture the scandal between the gypsy and the Baroness," he thought, "the chef crossed the line into excess. Too much chocolate is too much chocolate, no matter the social context." The next thought changed his life. "My family is excessive. There's mother's dancing at the Medzhybizh Town Hall. Her time breathing with Miss Sipos at the Király Baths. Even her extreme feelings of satisfaction. My sister is excessively beautiful from being formed in an unnatural womb. There's the excessiveness of my father's breakdown. When I walked into the shop, I entered the excessiveness of his madness." Isaak paused to let it sink in. "I didn't just sell cakes. They spoke through me. People couldn't just purchase my pastries. They had to be transformed. I had to be the excessive cake seller. I don't want to carry on my family's legacy anymore. I want my own life."

By now, we understand that Cake-analysis ultimately rests on the seller's commitment to self-discovery. Or, to put it another way, it is only by exploring themselves that the shop owner can find the customer. Now he had realised his own excessiveness, Isaak could have worked in a firm, yet quiet, manner. He no longer needed the thrill of cakes being smashed, floors being pissed on, or women getting goosebumps.

In that moment, Isaak understood he would never find another place that offered as much opportunity for self-knowledge as Cake-analysis. He may even have continued in the profession if Aliza had not thundered back into the store. She said, "Well! What does the Rigó Jancsi mean for you?"

"I don't want to be the next in my family to live a life of excess."

Very slowly, so each word stood alone, Aliza said, "That's fucking unbelievable." She shook her head, dismissing the pathetic thing before her. "Give me another Jancsi. There's a park next to the Hungarian Academy of Sciences. Maybe a young man will come and share it with me. I'll be his Baroness. He'll be my gypsy." She picked up the cake. "I'll send him to pay for it. He'll tell you what a bargain he's getting."

Isaak was not affected by Aliza's anger. She was no longer the issue. He had understood he had been living his family's life and now had to create his own—with Aliza, or without her. He knew exactly what to do.

For centuries, cakes were no more than bread that had been sweetened with dried fruits and nuts. They looked rough and their texture was abrasive.

At the beginning of the nineteenth century, chefs discovered they could make cakes smoother by adding cocoa. These new pastries were called velvet cakes.

Cocoa not only made cakes silkier, it also gave them a reddish tinge. Some bakers amplified the colouring by adding beetroot juice. This pastry was so popular with Americans in the early years of the twentieth century, they claimed the Red Velvet Cake as their own.

Isaak placed the Red Velvet on the right side of the Rigó Jancsi, on the bottom shelf. He then positioned the Punch Cake to the left of the Rigó. "Mrs Davidovitis," he said to himself, "Berko believed he could be the mad turkey without the angry Red Velvet. Have all the fun and sex you want. But you can't escape anger. Otherwise, you're just playing at being happy."

Isaak imagined a triumphant young fellow coming to pay for Aliza's purchase. Isaak would tell him, "To be the right man for Aliza, you have to be the whole display. Being her Rigó Jancsi is not enough." He would punch him, just to make the point. He'd throw a solid upper cut, followed by a booming right hook. "Thank you, Mr Kubrinszky. My training has finished. I'm ready for the ring."

That evening, scattered cloud sat in the sky above Budapest. Sometimes the light of the setting sun fell on one of the Synagogue's towers. That column would then fall into the shade, while the other shone brightly. There were moments when the sun lit part of one tower, while the rest remained in shadow. "The scene keeps changing and capturing the eye," Isaak thought. "That's what the best windows, and the best people, do. They don't fall into the Chocolate Chestnut Roulade rut." He then turned to his sister and said, "Shoshana, would you eat a Rigó Jancsi Chocolate Mousse Cake for love?"

"You know, all my life I assumed I was the gypsy. Up on stage, everybody wanting me. I'd now like to be the Baroness and risk the humiliation of throwing myself at someone. I have to stop being the Anonymous Statue if I'm going to join Vörösmarty's families."

"Mrs Davidovitis transformed the display window," Isaak said, "but her presentation is not as revolutionary as she thinks. I made some changes. I'm getting the hang of this cake business, but I still want out. I'd like a normal life. No excess."

"That sounds like a great idea."

17 🎂 The Marriage of Isaak Brodsky and Aliza Lövy

Isaak Brodsky had a plan as he entered the shop the next morning. He believed if he spent one day as a normal cake seller, he could then transition to an ordinary life. He would ask his customers about their morning coffee and discuss the flowers at Klauzál tér.

Despite everything Mrs Davidovitis had taught him, it did not occur to Isaak that if he wanted thoughtless conversations with his customers, he had to create a mindless display. In fact, by rearranging the bottom shelf the previous day, he had put himself into the window, giving it more power over him. The only way to save himself was to do something silly, like place the Hussar Kisses in the centre of the middle tier.

Of course, even an act as radical as resurrecting the Kisses may not have been enough. Is it really possible to be thoughtfully thoughtless? Wouldn't the underlying thinking shine through? Given everything he had experienced, was it still conceivable that Isaak could be an ordinary cake seller? I suspect his only option was to run for his life and hope for the best, as his father had done.

Mr László Goldziher had a thick beard that framed the serious face of a studious young man. Like most thinkers, he was thin and lanky, as if his active mind burnt through his calories. He walked to the counter and asked for a slice of Fruit Flan. He said, "I usually buy a layer cake, but that suddenly seems conservative. What could be more spontaneous than eating a Flan? It's not only French, with all those colours, it's positively gaudy."

The foundation of the Fruit Flan is a circular base of light pastry, turned up at the edges. The filling is a mixture of cream, cream cheese, sugar and vanilla. However, all this is simply superstructure for the brightly coloured fruits, spread randomly across the surface and covered in glaze.

When Keila Davidovitis placed the Flan to the far left of the bottom shelf, she'd said, "This cake is so at odds with the usual blacks, browns and whites of Hungarian pastries, I have no idea how to incorporate it into the display. But every window must have a cake that's searching for its place. It mirrors what your customers are trying to do. They'll buy it by the cart load."

Isaak knew all he had to do was give the Flan to László while telling him it was an excellent choice. Instead, he said, "The Fruit Flan looks like it's been thrown together on a whim. However, a great deal of thought goes into the selection and placement of the fruits. It's haphazard by design. It represents free expression, tempered by measured constraint. I suspect you have an expansive mind, László, but you'll only reach your full potential when you learn to practise restraint." Isaak finally managed to stop himself talking. He said, "I'm stuck in the Chocolate Chestnut Roulade. I keep going round and round, making these cake interpretations."

"But what if the Austrians are right?" said László. "It's not about walking purposefully up Andrássy. It's wandering around the Ringstrasse. What if the Roulade is exactly the right cake? It tells us everything is part of a never-ending cycle. Top shelf, bottom shelf, it's all an illusion."

"You can see all that?"

"Yes, it's in the presentation. Each cake is a transitional point to the next. But no pastry is ultimately the end. The window is infinite."

"Like my mother and Miss Sipos breathing naked at the Király Baths? I couldn't cope with that."

"I have no idea what you're talking about. Though it sounds exciting. This window sets the mind free. The previous display was too crazy. It overwhelmed the brain, stopping you from thinking. It was like the seller was trying to keep you out of the shop. And all those mindless presentations around the quarter. They're wilfully finite. You buy the same cake over and over again, as if you have no choice. I'm going to stay and eat my Flan. Something big is going to happen here today."

A group of students were passing the store. László called them in and told them to buy a slice of Fruit Flan. When he suggested a momentous event was about to occur, they responded, "A revolution in a cake shop.

How Hungarian. How Jewish."

Isaak Brodsky was worried that things were getting out of hand. He said, "Mr Goldziher, you and your friends must take your cakes outside. We need space for others to enter."

László said, "There's plenty of room."

"It's not how many can fit in the store. It's how many can fit in the cake seller's mind. Right now, that's not many."

"Isaak, I keep telling you the window's too big for one person's brain. You'll always be a step behind the cakes."

"But things could spin out of control."

"You took that risk when you included the Flan in the display. Only a madman would do that."

Nobody really knows how things work at these points. When are we acknowledging the magic of the world and when are we slipping into magical thinking? Why did a group of old ladies, none of whom had previously visited Brodsky's, enter at that moment? Did the window speak to them? Or was it coincidence?

Mrs Cohen was clearly the leader of the elderly women. She said, "Young man. We're here to let our hair down. Give us all the Mandelbrot you've got. We'll take them to the park by the Hungarian Academy of Sciences and stuff ourselves silly."

"No ladies," said Isaak. "I cannot sell you the Mandelbrot. You might have a great time at Széchenyi István tér, but that purchase will ultimately leave you feeling empty. It will be the beginning of the end."

"Should we have Apple Strudel?"

"That would be worse."

"Then what could it possibly be?"

I would love to wax lyrical about how we had reached the point The Interpretation of Cakes had always been heading toward. I could eulogise that having finally understood he would never be bigger than the cakes, Isaak let himself metaphorically fall forward, as his mother had done when she was caught by Miss Sipos at the Király Baths. I could gush that this submission allowed him to become both the creator of the window, and the window. Or, from a psychotherapy perspective, in freeing the mind of the patient, he freed himself. Or, where László Goldziher had introduced him to the limitlessness of the display, Isaak was discovering the limitlessness of his brain. The truth is, Isaak was just overwhelmed. Still, it did not matter that Isaak's surrender came from defeat, rather than acceptance. His unconscious had won the battle. It was free to create his world.

Isaak's psyche produced an image of him sitting at the Auguszt Café. He saw himself calling out, "Apple Strudel." Someone yelled, "Silk Road." Another, "The Turks." He said to Mrs Cohen, "You must have Baklava!"

"Baklava! So risqué! But you don't sell it."

"It doesn't matter. You don't actually need the cake for it to help you, in the psychological sense. Ask Hershko Kubrinszky, if you don't believe me. That man's wise beyond his years."

"Yes, but we're just here for cake. Not in the psychological sense. Whatever that means."

"Mrs Cohen, no one just goes to a shop for cake, even though patisserie owners try to convince their customers otherwise. Everybody needs to be understood."

"I'm glad we've cleared that up. We'll go over and eat our non-existent Baklava with those young people. Can I point out they're actually eating Fruit Flans?"

Isaak handed Mrs Cohen a number of Apple Strudels. "Here's your Baklava."

"Oh, look at these Turkish sweets," said Mrs Cohen. "I'm so glad you didn't sell us that silly old Mandelbrot."

Isaak gently waved the women toward the students. "Those youngsters are good value. Go and have fun with them."

When the old ladies joined the scholars, Mrs Cohen said, "Tell me this, Mr Goldziher. What happened when the traders on the Silk Road got to the end of their journey and sold their wares?"

"They bought goods to take back home to sell."

"Then what?"

"They did it all over again."

"Round and round, slowly changing the world."

"I've always thought it was straight lines. I now understand it's circles."

"Does that mean one day we'll end up back with the Mandelbrot?"

"Yes, but you'll be different. And the Mandelbrot will have changed."

A group of angry men burst into the shop. Their leader, Mr Katzburg, leaned threateningly across the counter. He said, "There's nowhere to go for time out since your father left. Look at my friends. They try to smile but they can't do it. They're affecting everyone. Bit by bit, the quarter's grin is becoming a grimace. Now you've changed the window. You're telling us we have no place."

Nina came into the shop carrying a tray of Syrniki. She walked to the counter and asked Isaak what was wrong. "Whenever I get somewhere," he answered, "I end up nowhere. Look at these angry men."

"This is wonderful," Nina said. "I wondered why I had to cook these cakes, especially after deciding to never bake again. Now I can see I've been given another chance to be a big Kugelhopf breast. Both to you and these poor fellows. Thank you, Isaak. You're amazing." Nina offered the Syrniki to Mr Katzburg's group. She said, "These are the pastries my mother used to make. They're filled with love."

The men were not wanting to metaphorically sit on the porch overlooking the lake at Medzhybizh. They wanted everybody to know how unfairly life had treated them. They had escaped the violence of the pogroms, only to be imprisoned in a world of happiness. They screamed that Syrniki is a stupid cake that should have been left in Ukraine. "And you're a stupid woman for offering it to us," Mr Katzburg yelled.

Nina stood calmly, holding her Syrniki out in front of her. She said soothing things. "I know it's hard. I understand why you want nothing to do with the Syrniki." The group snarled at her.

Meanwhile, Mrs Cohen said to László, "For me, the Indian Head has always been a foolish cake. Now, I see that it tells us to purchase the Theatre de Wein and live our lives. You could end up looking like a goose, but still do something good." She took the Indian Head from the top shelf and swapped it with the Rigó Jancsi, in the centre of the bottom tier.

"That's good," said Mr Goldziher, "but what about the Punch Cake. It might be the pastry of fun, but it also reminds us of the anarchist bakers out at Kozma utca Cemetery and their endless tantrums, all in the hope of changing the world. They're the real geese."

"Let's place the Esterházy next to the Punch Cake," said Mrs Cohen. "If Anton III threw the odd fit, things might have turned out differently."

"That's true," said László. "Being the decent man eating the good solid Kipfel didn't help him."

Keila Davidovitis had reached Brodsky's just as László Goldziher placed the Punch Cake in the centre of the bottom shelf. She watched through the window as Mrs Cohen repositioned the Esterházy Cream Torte. Keila was pleased with what she saw. "A successful window must be constantly changing," she thought. She then noticed Nina Brodsky was surrounded by a group of infuriated men. She quickly made her way inside and moved the Red Velvet Cake to the centre of the bottom shelf. She called loudly, "An angry cake for angry people."

Mr Katzburg came over to Keila. "Thank you," he said. "All we ever needed was someone to say it's alright to be furious." He looked back at the enraged mob and nodded. They all took a Syrniki from Nina.

Mr Katzburg turned to Mrs Davidovitis and said, "May I?"

"Of course."

Mr Katzburg placed the Syrniki next to the Red Velvet Cake.

"It's as if those two pastries were made for each other," said Keila.

Mr Katzburg flung his arms around Keila Davidovitis. He gestured for Nina to join them. All the customers merged into a group hug. Isaak came from behind the counter. His mother kissed him on the cheek and whispered, "I love you."

Mrs Davidovitis said, "We all do."

Nina said, "We need to dance."

"Mother!" Isaak said.

"Not like the Medzhybizh Town Hall. No touching."

One of the things I learnt from my practice was when things are going bad, they tend to get worse. The opposite is also true. Good things pile up, one on top of the other, in ways that are hard to believe. The job of the therapist is to hold the patient through the hard times, while helping them to make the inner changes that will ultimately transform their lives. Get this right, and their world changes. Unexpected things happen.

Hershko Kubrinszky came into the shop, followed by a number of musicians. He said, "I went to a bar last night for the first time in my life. I was looking for a Punch Cake experience." He laughed. "The band was playing Klezmer music. I told them to bring their instruments to this shop.

We've come to rejoice in what you've created, Isaak."

"But it was Mrs Davidovitis who changed the presentation," said Isaak. "Look at all these people. Things have moved on. I'm left in her wake."

"Mrs Davidovitis did an excellent job. But we all know nothing would have happened if you hadn't told me to buy a Punch Cake.

"But that was the pastries."

"You still had to let them speak through you."

"That was because I didn't have enough of a self to stop them."

"I didn't come here to get stuck in a Roulade argument. Anyway, the musicians are ready to begin."

The fiddler started to play. He sounded deliberately off key, as if he was both settling into the tune and rebelling against it. The clarinet player joined at an edgy pitch that was both exciting and slightly irritating. Then came the accordion, followed by the hammered dulcimer.

The customers formed two circles, one male, one female. The dancers lifted their arms in the air and grasped their neighbours' hands. They moved in a clockwise direction, first placing their right foot in front of the left. Then the left foot was pushed as far to the left as was comfortable. Then the right foot went behind the left. As the dancers moved, they swayed their bodies from side to side, or let their knees bend, allowing them to dip.

Mr Kubrinszky moved to the centre of the men's circle. With his arms crossed in front of his chest, he squatted and threw his legs out in front of him. The band increased the tempo. The other dancers let go of each other's hands and clapped. Hershko danced faster. The band quickened its pace, drawing him further into the pleasure of the movement. He looked around the smiling faces and realised he had finally left Angyalföld. He saw Isaak was again standing behind the counter. He kissed the middle fingers of his right hand and flung it at him.

Hershko wanted to keep going, revelling in the moment. The other dancers would have happily given him the floor. It is not every day you witness a man leave Angyalföld. Hershko felt generous. There would be more times when he would experience this joy. He fell back into the circle. Mr Katzburg danced into the centre.

Over in the women's circle, Nina held centre stage. She kept her arms above her head, and let her hips sway from side to side. Nina was making her own discoveries. She missed the sexual anarchy of the Medzhybizh Town Hall. She longed for Miss Sipos's touch at the Király Baths. At the same time, she revelled in her body finding its own rhythm. She too could have kept dancing.

Nina fell back to the circle, next to Keila. She yelled, "Thank you for what you've done for our family. Your tears and pee might not have watered Margit Island, but they certainly helped us flower."

"It's a pleasure, Mrs Brodsky. I hope you'll wet yourself one day."

"I think I already have. In my own way."

Nina moved Keila into the centre of the circle, then withdrew and went up to the flat.

Isaak desperately wanted to dance but he knew there was one last Cake-analytic job he had to do. Aliza would return and he had to be ready. He decided he would make a simple statement. "Miss Lövy, the Rigó Jancsi is the couple's cake. The gypsy and the Baroness were an odd pair who managed to find each other. That's what the cake means to me. I'm ready to be part of a relationship."

Isaak suddenly realised the band had stopped playing. He looked up and saw his sister and Aliza standing before him. He had no idea when everything had gone quiet.

Shoshana said, "Isaak, I woke up this morning and thought you had given me so much, I wanted to do something for you. I walked over to the Kazinczy Synagogue and found Aliza in tears. She turned to me and yelled, 'The shul lied about being Orthodox and art nouveau. And what's wrong with those Secessionists? I'm sure the Ringstrasse's beautiful.'

"I said I was sorry she was upset, but would she come to the shop and give you another chance. I agreed that you are an oddball, a bit of an Indian Head. But you have brought life and joy to our family. We arrived just in time to hear your beautiful speech."

"I didn't realise I was talking aloud."

"You were, and you can't blame this one on the cakes."

Isaak looked past Shoshana to see his mother had brought his father to the shop. "I dragged him out of the pantry," Nina called. "We got here just as you started speaking."

Mr Katzburg walked over to Yaakov and shook his hand. "We've been struggling since you left," he said. "But leaving the shop was obviously a good decision. You look very relaxed."

Yaakov thanked Mr Katzburg, then said, "Excuse me. There's something I have to do."

Yaakov went to the baking room and retrieved two chairs. Isaak and Aliza were each placed in a seat, then lifted into the air by four men. The band started playing and the couple were carried around the shop, their chairs lifting and falling, as the others danced around them. From time to time, they were close enough to hold hands. Mostly, they were apart. Everyone sang, "Siman tov, Mazel tov."

The dancing finished and Isaak made his first ever speech. He thanked everyone for coming and the band for playing so enthusiastically. He acknowledged Keila and Hershko for moulding him into a Cake-analyst. He thanked his family for never giving up on him. He thanked Aliza for being a Secessionist determined to be both Orthodox and art nouveau. He said he would try to be a good husband, doing the best he could, but never going to extremes. "Finally, I want to thank the cakes. Without them, we would never have escaped the Chocolate Chestnut Roulade."

Isaak Brodsky never went back to the shop.

🎂 Epilogue

Isaak and Aliza would have been in their late forties when Germany invaded Hungary in 1944, and started deporting Jews to Auschwitz. It was likely they had children. They may have had grandchildren. I could not leave Budapest until I knew if they survived.

I found myself walking to the Kazinczy Synagogue and staring at the Stars of David. I sat in City Park by the Anonymous Statue. I visited the poet in Vörösmarty tér and ingested fine cakes at Gerbeauds. I sat in the warm waters of the Király Baths, letting the breath run through my body. I joined the mad turkeys at the Auguszt Café. I would yell, "Brodsky," invariably bringing the free associations to a halt.

I obviously spent time in Rumbach utca. From what I could work out, there was now a café where Brodsky's used to be. I often ate at that restaurant. In an odd way, it felt like home. I would ask the person who served me if they knew of Brodsky's Fine Cakes and Biscuits from the early years of last century. They were always courteous, but had no idea what I was talking about.

I finally returned to Australia, but could not let the family go. About eight hundred Hungarian Jewish refugees made it to Sydney during the war. Many settled in the city's eastern suburbs. Some families still ran patisseries. I went to that part of town most days.

It was only to be expected that I would order a Flódni, the little cake that always seemed on the verge of collapse. I sometimes felt I was the wrong man in the wrong place with the wrong story and bought an Indian Head. Then there were the moments when I felt lonely and purchased a Rigó Jancsi Chocolate Mousse Cake, hoping someone would find me and we would form a couple. I began to worry that I was sliding into a Chocolate Chestnut Roulade rut where I would play out this ritual for the rest of my life. The day came when I ordered a Dobos Torte.

I suspect the young man behind the counter had been watching me. He said, "The Dobos would be a backward step. You should buy a Punch Cake. You need to have more fun."

I was staggered, but managed to say, "Watch out! I might squash it and storm out. Then you'll never be rid of me."

The young man laughed.

I asked, "What's your name?"

"Bruce."

"No, your surname."

"Yes, Bruce."

"That's your Anglicised name. What's your family's Hungarian name?"

"I think you know."

I stumbled out to the street and started to cry.

I still spend my time in the park that overlooks the spot where Sydney Harbour transforms into the Parramatta River. I see my grandmother sweating in the Australian heat as she bakes the Christmas Cakes and Puddings that will make our day special. I sit with my family on a headland, eating Cream Buns as we watch the surf roll in. I now understand the message of those cakes. We don't have a lot to give, we don't even know how unworldly we are, but we love you and are doing our best.

Acknowledgements

Andy Kissane's help and support has been crucial in getting this book to publication. My partner, Risé Becker, has lived with all my frustrations. Over the years, a number of readers have given me valuable feedback. These include Adrian Ford, Anthea Lowe, Carmel Flaskas, Howard Gwynn, Libby Dunn, Louise Marsden, Marice Lieberman and Pam Christie.

I have found the following books invaluable for my research. *Ultimate Cake*, Barbara Maher, DK Publishing, New York, 1996; *Encyclopedia of Jewish Food*, Gil Marks, John Wiley and Sons, Hoboken, 2010; *Treasure Trove of Hungarian Cookery*, Maria Vizári, Corvina Kiadó, Budapest, 1961.

www.ingramcontent.com/pod-product-compliance
Lightning Source LLC
Chambersburg PA
CBHW031240260626
47169CB00007B/2392